A SUB TO L

Club of Dominance 4

Becca Van

MENAGE EVERLASTING

Siren Publishing, Inc.
www.SirenPublishing.com

A SIREN PUBLISHING BOOK
IMPRINT: Ménage Everlasting

A SUB TO LOVE
Copyright © 2013 by Becca Van

ISBN: 978-1-62740-602-4

First Printing: November 2013

Cover design by Harris Channing
All art and logo copyright © 2013 by Siren Publishing, Inc.

Printed in the U.S.A.

PUBLISHER
Siren Publishing, Inc.
www.SirenPublishing.com

A SUB TO LOVE

Club of Dominance 4

BECCA VAN
Copyright © 2013

Chapter One

"Jesus." Derrick Jackson jumped, startled when the door to his office opened, ripping him from his thoughts. He looked up from where he sat at the receptionist desk to see who'd disturbed him. While he and his brother, Garth, had posted an ad for a new administrative assistant almost a month ago, Derrick definitely hadn't expected a woman like this to walk through the front door. She headed across the waiting room, right toward him, and moved with such a fluid feminine grace his breath caught in his throat and his heart stuttered. Never had he seen such sensual womanly elegance in his life. Whoever she was, she had him spellbound and that never happened to Derrick, at least it never had before now. Her hair was so black it had a tint of blue from the gleam of the light above. She was slim and lithe but curvy in all the right places, and she had stormy gray eyes with skin so creamy white it was almost translucent. Her lips were full and formed into a natural pout, and he could just imagine that sweet, sexy mouth wrapped around his cock. He rose to his feet as she came closer, and he saw her eyes widen as she seemed to take in his full six-foot-six height and muscular body. Her steps hesitated for a fraction of a second and she looked away as her white skin began to tinge with pink.

Is she intimidated by me or does she like what she's seeing?

She stopped in front of the desk, glanced into his eyes and then quickly looked away again.

"May I help you?"

"Yes." She licked her lips nervously. "I have an appointment with a Mr. Garth Jackson. My name is Justine Downey."

Derrick moved out from behind the counter and held his hand out to her. "I'm Derrick Jackson, Miss Downey. I'm pleased to meet you."

"Mr. Jackson," she said breathily and took his hand.

If Derrick hadn't been watching her so intently, he might have missed her reaction as their hands clasped. She drew in a deep breath and her pupils widened. Warmth raced up his arm and centered in his chest, and his cock twitched behind the zipper of his pants. Justine pressed her lips together in a tight line but then those beautiful red bows parted as she exhaled. Derrick moved his fingers to her wrist as he went to withdraw his hand, the tips skimming over her rapid pulse. She shivered visibly. He took a step back as she lowered her eyes to the floor, giving her space to regain her equilibrium.

So submissive and unaware.

"Please follow me into the office." Derrick indicated the office he shared with Garth and waited for Justine to lead the way. He could tell she was uncomfortable at having him behind her by the tension in her scrunched shoulders and taut neck, but not once did she hesitate in her step.

Garth rose to his feet as they entered and walked out from behind his desk as he eyed Justine Downey. Derrick could see the interest in his brother's eyes when Garth shifted his gaze to his and raised an eyebrow in silent question.

"Ms. Downey, this is my brother, Garth." Derrick then swept a hand toward one of the chairs in front of their two desks. Derrick dragged a chair from across the room and placed it in front of her and sat down to face her, but so that he was sitting close enough to reach out and touch her and Garth did the same with the other chair so he was next to him but also facing Justine and within touching distance. He heard her inhale and then try to exhale quietly with unease, but she still offered Garth her hand in greeting and again Derrick watched her for a reaction. He had to clench his jaw hard to keep a satisfied smile from forming on his face when she reacted the same way to Garth as she had to him.

"May I call you Justine?" Garth asked.

"Certainly, I'm not a big fan of titles and such. I've always thought that respect should be earned, not demanded."

"My thoughts exactly," Derrick agreed. "Please, call us Derrick and Garth."

Justine nodded.

"I've read over your resume, Justine. It's quite impressive. While you've never worked in the security business before, all your other experience seems compatible, and I think you would be perfect for the job. Do you have any questions?" Garth glanced at Derrick and by the look in his eye, Derrick could tell that his brother had picked up on Justine's reaction to their handshake.

"I would like an employment contract to read over the job description before I decide whether to take the job or not."

Garth rose to his feet and walked over to his desk and then picked up some papers and brought them over to Justine.

"Thank you." She took the papers and glanced over them.

"Would you like something to drink while you're reading the contract?" Derrick moved toward the door but paused while he awaited a reply.

"Coffee would be nice, thanks."

Derrick headed to the kitchen in the back of the building. When he entered, he was grateful that there was still warm coffee left from earlier and that he wouldn't have to be away from Justine for so long, while he waited for more coffee to brew. He poured the coffee into three mugs and placed them on a tray with cream and sugar.

Justine didn't glance toward him when he entered the office again, but from the color on her cheeks she was very aware of Garth's and his presence. Garth was still sitting in the chair across from her and he'd guess hadn't removed his eyes from the gorgeous woman.

"How do you take your coffee?" Derrick asked.

She looked up at him. "Cream only, please."

He waited until she finished reading through the contract before handing her the mug. "So what do you think?"

"Everything seems to be in order. When would you like me to start?" Justine sipped her coffee and closed her eyes as if savoring the taste.

She was a very sensual woman and judging from the way she moved naturally and without any guile, she had no idea how sexy she was. Derrick's cock was hard and his balls were aching. The urge to pick her up and cradle her in his arms was so strong he had to clench his hands so hard that his knuckles ached to prevent himself from following through with his needs.

"You can start now, if you would like." Garth's voice drew him back from his desire-induced trance.

"Okay. That's acceptable, but I have to make a call first. I share a house with my…brother, and he was expecting me back. If I don't return, he'll be upset."

Derrick frowned over the hesitation and fear he heard in her voice when she spoke of her brother. She was a grown woman, why would her brother be upset if she didn't come home? Why would she fear her own sibling? Something seemed off, but he knew he had no right to question her. He glanced over at Garth and saw concern on his brother's face. He'd obviously picked up on her fear, too. *What the hell is going on?*

"Do you have a pen I could use?" Justine asked.

Derrick took the opportunity to turn away from her to regain his composure. He drew in a deep breath and exhaled slowly and then he turned around and handed her the pen.

"Thanks." Justine used her thigh to brace the contract, filled in her personal details, and signed. "Okay who is going to give me a rundown on how things work here?"

"I will." Garth rose to his feet and swept out a hand toward the office door. "Let me show you around first and after that we'll give you a crash course on how we like things done."

Derrick watched the sensual sway of her sexy rounded hips. His hard cock jerked against the zipper of his pants and he reached down to adjust the fit of his jeans. He was going to be damned uncomfortable walking around the office with a constant hard-on.

* * * *

Garth led Justine to the back of the building to the control room, where the, security systems were being monitored. Luke and Matt Plant were working this shift, but he was wary about introducing her to those two Doms. There was no way they wouldn't pick up on her submissiveness. Just as he and Derrick had.

He and his brother had been frequenting Club of Dominance for years and had hoped to meet the sub of their dreams, one they could share between them, but that hadn't happened. Justine was a sub through and through and had no idea of her proclivity to be dominated. He would love to take her to the club and introduce her to the wonders of BDSM, but she was an employee, so he didn't think that would ever happen. Pushing his lustful thoughts aside, he hoped Matt and Luke didn't see what was obvious.

He opened the door to the back room and stayed close to her side. This protectiveness he was feeling toward her bothered him. He'd always looked out for the weaker sex and stepped in to protect them if the situation arose, but he'd never felt so…possessive before. Garth guided her across the room, being careful not to touch her. He'd already picked up on her nervousness and how she tried to keep her personal space clear, so he respected her needs and didn't get too close or touch her.

Matt and Luke turned toward them and the brothers immediately perused Justine's body. Their interest was obvious. A gleam appeared in Matt's eyes when Justine looked away from them and then down to the floor. Garth noted that her hands were clasped behind her back, and he wondered if she had experience with the BDSM lifestyle.

"Guys, this is our new office assistant, Justine Downey. Justine, this is Luke and Matt Plant."

"It's a pleasure, Justine. I hope you like working here." Matt held out his hand and although she hesitated, she shook it.

"Welcome aboard, darlin'." Luke also shook her hand. "These guys are great bosses but if you have any trouble, you come to us and we'll sort them out."

"What?" Justine frowned and then stepped back.

Luke held up his hands, palms out. "I was just mucking around, Justine. No one here would ever do anything inappropriate or hurt you."

The tension that had invaded Justine's shoulders diminished a little and they slumped in relief. *What the hell? What has been done to her to make her so wary?*

Derrick moved to the side and began to explain about their back-to-base security systems and how they had employees monitoring the systems at all times. "We have a constant rotation of staff to look after the equipment so there are people in and out of here all day and night. We'll introduce you to everyone as they come on shift. Most of our employees come in through the rear door. No one can get in unless their thumbprint has been put into the computer system. The only public access to the building is the front door you came in through."

"Good to know," Justine said. "What happens if an alarm is tripped?"

"We have a direct line to the police and call it in," Matt explained, "but everyone who works here is also trained to go out and take care of any criminals."

Justine turned to look at him. "Wow, you have quite a setup."

"Yes, we do," Garth said. "We also have security officers out on patrol keeping an eye on things. As you can see from the monitors, we can see a lot of streets and if the guys watching the screens see anything suspicious, they can send in someone to check it out. We've stopped a lot of criminals before they gained entry to properties illegally."

"And the police are okay with this?"

"Yes," Garth answered honestly. "The cops have enough to deal with and if we can make their jobs easier…well, they appreciate it."

"I can imagine."

"Okay, let me show you where we keep our client files and employee records." Garth led Justine out of the control room to the filing room. Once done showing her where everything was, he guided her back to the reception area. "I'll get you some brochures and you can read through them. That way when a potential client asks you any questions, you'll be able to answer them."

"Thank you," Justine nodded and sat down in the chair. "I would really appreciate that."

Garth walked to his office and grabbed the manual on all their products, glad for a moment to take a deep breath. Justine's light flowery scent had curled around his cock and balls and hadn't let go. He was aching for relief but knew there would be none anytime soon. He handed over the product information and then headed back to the office. He had a shitload of e-mails to get through. The office work was his least favorite part of the job. He'd rather be out installing the systems than cooped up in the office. The fact that he and Derrick had found a means to put their former military experience to use in a way that could help protect citizens was often the consolation that got him through the long hours at his desk.

He heard Justine on the phone and wondered if she was calling her brother. He still didn't understand why a woman in her early twenties had to check in with her brother. A knot formed in his gut, his instincts on high alert. One thing he had learned whilst in the military was to never discount a gut reaction. Doing so had saved his life a time or two.

"Mark, I won't be home until late this afternoon, I was lucky enough to get the job and they wanted me to start immediately. Do you have a pen? I'll give you the phone number, and you can call if you need to contact me in an emergency."

Garth looked over at Derrick and found his brother frowning at Justine's back. He'd heard the anxiety in her voice, too. She rattled off the office number and then slumped into the chair while listening to her brother's response.

"Shit, can't you cook your own dinner for a change? It's not like you and that friend of yours have anything pressing to do." Garth could hear the agitation in her voice and really wished he could hear the other end of the conversation. When she sighed resignedly before lowering her voice as if she didn't want to be overheard, his ears perked up and his gut began to churn. "Okay, I'll cook dinner when I get home, but you and Bart have to clean up."

Garth wanted to respect her wishes for privacy, but with his alarm bells ringing, he wasn't about to relent. She worked for them now and as far as he was concerned she was under their protection. He would do anything to keep her safe but most of all he wanted her to be happy. Her stormy-gray eyes had such sad depths to them and he wanted to be able to change that. The anger in her voice drew his attention once more.

"Why the hell do you have to go out tonight? You and Bart go out every night. Can't you just pitch in a little? I've been the only one bringing in an income for the last five years and doing all the chores. Why can't you stay home and clean up for a change?"

Garth wished Justine didn't have her back to him. He liked to be able to see a sub's face and gauge their reactions, although Justine's body language was readable enough from behind. Her shoulders were tense and scrunched up toward her neck and her voice gave her away. She wasn't happy and he didn't blame her one little bit. Anger ran through him at the thought of her having to take care of earning the money and doing all the other chores. He wondered how old her brother was. Maybe he was just a teenager and she had been taking care of him.

Are her parents still alive? If they had died, then the responsibility of raising a young teenager would have been tough. But if he was a young man, he needed to have his ass kicked. And why was the brother's friend living with them?

"I'm sorry. Forget I asked. I'll see you when I get home."

Justine placed the phone down gently. That she hadn't lost control was a conundrum to him. It seemed that Justine Downey kept a tight rein on herself, even if her body language suggested she had wanted to slam the receiver down.

Would she ever totally let go if I topped her?

Garth really wanted to know the answer to that question and since he and his brother were very attracted to her, he hoped he got the chance to find out. But how long would it take them to get her to relax around them?

Chapter Two

As Justine settled into her place at the receptionist desk, she couldn't keep her mind from focusing on the Jackson brothers. She had never been more aware of a man, or men, as she was of those two.

They were freaking huge and so damn good looking her panties were wet.

Derrick stood well over six feet and made her feel like a kid in his presence. He towered over her, and because of his height and bulk she was a little intimidated. He had short dark brown hair, the most soulful brown eyes she had ever seen and lightly tanned skin. His brother, Garth, was a couple of inches shorter than Derrick but he was still hellishly tall for a man. His hair was a lighter shade of brown, almost amber, and his eyes were hazel. They were both brawny and ripped with muscle and the aura of power around them drew her to them like a moth to a flame. But she had learned that men were all lazy assholes and had no intention of getting burned.

Her brother, Mark, had taught her as much, anyway. They'd been the only family each other had for the twelve years since her parents were killed during the September Eleventh attacks. Mark was five years older than her and should have been helping her carry the financial burden, but instead he'd never worked a day in his life, unless she counted the work that went into making the messes she had to clean up once she got home.

The phone on her desk rang and she reached for it. "Jackson Security, Justine speaking."

"Hello, Jus."

"Bart, why are you calling me at work?"

"You need to get some food before you come home. We had a few friends over to watch the game. You know how it is."

Justine shivered as his slick, oily voice caused her muscles to tense. She didn't like Bart one bit. In fact he downright frightened her. The fact that he had decided to move into her home rent-free five years ago and had yet to vacate meant she never got a break from him or his lecherous grins every time she passed him in the hallway.

But to avoid making a bad impression at her new job, she suppressed her boiling anger and replied, "I can't get any food, Bart. I don't have any money left. I only bought groceries three days ago and that should have been enough to last for the rest of the week."

"Come on, Jus, don't get mad. You know we like to watch sports with our friends."

"Look, Bart, I don't care what you like. If we need more food, then you and Mark are going to have to go out and get it. Don't call me at work again unless there is an emergency." Justine hung up the phone and hoped her new bosses hadn't heard her. The deep voice behind her filled her with dread.

"Everything okay, Justine?"

Justine looked up into Derrick's brown eyes. Another shiver worked its way up her spine, but this time for a totally different reason.

"Yes, thanks. I'm sorry for the personal call. Hopefully it won't happen again."

"I don't care about the call, honey, but I do care that you are upset."

"I'm fine, but thanks anyway." Justine looked away. She wasn't fine at all and couldn't lie worth a damn. Her parents had instilled good morals into her and Mark, and that was one of the reasons she couldn't understand her brother's lazy attitude. They hadn't been brought up to be lazy or to expect everything to be handed to them on a platter.

"Okay, but if you ever need to talk, you can come to me or Garth."

Justine just nodded and then concentrated on the brochure again and was able to finally relax a little when he moved away.

By the end of the day, she was utterly exhausted. The awareness she had of Derrick and Garth had kept her on pins all day long. Just as she shut down the computer and switched the office phone to the answering machine, Luke and Matt Plant walked down the hall toward the desk.

"How was your first day, Justine?" Matt asked.

"It was good, thank you. I spent most of the time reading up on the security systems."

"Are you heading straight home?" Luke leaned against the reception desk.

"Yes." Justine glanced at her watch as she reached for her purse, which she'd stowed in a drawer. The next bus was due in ten minutes and if she missed that one, she would have to wait a half hour for the following one. She was going to have to hurry as it was, because the bus stop was a couple of blocks away. "I have to get going. It was nice meeting you both." She rounded the desk and was out the door moments later.

"Wait up, Justine," Luke called. "Can we give you a lift anywhere?"

"No thanks. I'll see you tomorrow." She hurried down the street. The Plant brothers were nearly as big as the Jacksons, but she wasn't drawn to them at all. She could see the interest in their eyes but had no intention of letting them get close to her. Justine wasn't interested in a relationship with any man. Not after living with her lazy-assed brother and friend for so long. Justine had begun to suspect that Mark and his deadbeat friend were on drugs. She'd never seen him taking anything but the niggling feeling that she was right wouldn't leave. She'd even come out and asked him point blank one day and he had adamantly refuted her question, but he hadn't been able to look her in the eye. She was sick and tired of dealing with his and Bart's mood swings and carrying the load. What she needed to do was find a place of her own so she didn't have to work herself to the bone all the time.

You would jump at the chance to have a relationship with one or both of the Jackson men. Stop lying to yourself, girl.

Shut up. Not only was she talking to herself, but she was answering, too. Maybe she was going crazy with exhaustion.

Justine was just in time to get on the bus. As it pulled away from the curb, she checked her purse. She had the grand total of twenty bucks left and that was supposed to last her the entire week. If Mark, Bart, and their friends had cleaned out the fridge and pantry then they were screwed. While she rode the bus, she tried to figure out what to buy to get them through until she got her first paycheck. Bread, eggs, and milk were a must. Protein was filling and so was bread. That would have to do. If Mark or Bart complained, she would tell them both to go to hell.

An hour later, Justine walked into the kitchen and put the small amount of groceries away. The house was quiet and she wondered if Mark and Bart had already gone out. God, she hoped so. It would be nice to spend the evening alone without them around. She walked into the living room and nearly screamed with frustration. Dishes covered every inch of the coffee table, the arms of the lounge had glasses on them, and the floor was also littered with crockery, crumbs, and papers. Sighing with frustration and the futility of getting angry, she began to clean up. She had just bent over to pick up three mugs off the floor when she heard a noise behind her.

Turning her head she saw blue denim jeans and was about to straighten when male hands gripped her hips painfully. She gasped when he shoved his denim-covered erection into her ass. Justine was so scared and shocked she fell to her hands and knees and scrambled away. When she was close to the sofa she used it to lever to her feet and turned to face Bart. "What the hell do you think you're doing?"

"It's just you and me, babe." Bart spread his arms wide and gave her a lewd smirk. "Why don't we go and have some fun?"

Justine edged her way along the front of the lounge and then skirted around the side and didn't stop until the large piece of furniture was between them.

"Where's Mark? I thought he wanted me to cook dinner for the both of you before you went out." Justine didn't like the lustful look in Bart's eyes and it made her skin crawl with fear.

"Plans have changed." Bart moved close to the front of the sofa and Justine stepped back. "There was something he had to do. He won't be back for a few hours."

Bart was five foot eleven and his body was turning to fat from lack of activity. He'd been drinking and she could smell the alcohol seeping through his pores. He moved slightly clockwise around the lounge, and she mimicked his movement, maintaining her distance as she looked for the best escape route. One led to the kitchen and the other led toward the hall. There was no way she was going to the kitchen. He would have her trapped if she did. She pushed off the lounge and hurried across the room. Once she reached the hall, she raced toward her bedroom. Besides the bathroom, her room was the only other one that had a lock on the door.

She was only a couple of yards away when hands gripped the back of her shirt. Justine screamed and fell headlong toward her door. She cried out when her eye and cheekbone connected with the hard metal handle, her cry of fear cut off as pain radiated into her face and head and then her hands and knees as she crashed to the floor. She cried out again when cruel hands flipped her over onto her back and then the front of her shirt was ripped open. Buttons flew and landed on the cold tile floor, making little pinging noises. Justine brought her knees up, using her feet and the strength in her legs, and tried to push Bart away. He raised his hand and was about to slap her in the face when she heard a key in the front door.

Bart quickly got to his feet and walked down the hall to meet her brother. Justine was shaking so much her limbs felt totally boneless and she didn't have the energy to get up off the floor. With a sob she pulled her shirt over her bra-clad breasts and stared at the two men who had been exploiting her for nearly five years.

"What the fuck is going on?" Mark yelled and tried to walk around Bart.

Bart grabbed Mark's shirt and twisted it in his fist. "Calm down, dude, it's not what it looks like. Justine tripped and hit her face on her bedroom door handle. I grabbed her shirt to try to help her up, but the buttons ripped off."

Mark pushed Bart aside and hurried over to her. He knelt down next to her and cupped her uninjured cheek. "Is that what happened, Jus?"

She looked at Bart over Mark's shoulder to see him glaring at her angrily. He was trying to intimidate her into not telling the truth. She wasn't about to let him get away with trying to rape her. This was an opportunity she wasn't going to let pass.

"No," she replied, her voice cracking with emotion. She took a deep steadying breath and then told her brother what really happened. Mark gripped her elbow and helped her to stand and then placed himself in front of her.

"That's it, man. Pack your stuff and get the fuck out. You think I haven't seen the way you looked at Jus? You need help, Bart. You're more fucked up than I am." Mark spun around to face her again. "Go into your room and lock the door. Don't come out until I come and get you. I'm sorry, Jus."

She glanced around Mark toward Bart and didn't like the fury she saw on the other man's face. Her brother was taller than Bart, but the asshole was at least thirty pounds heavier, albeit fat, not muscle. If they ended up physically fighting, Justine hoped that Mark was the stronger of the two. Justine hesitated but knew she wouldn't be a match to Bart if a fight started, so she went into her bedroom and locked herself in.

She stood with her ear pressed against the door, but she couldn't hear anything. When she moved to walk over to her bed, she heard a loud shout and then what sounded like a gunshot. Covering her mouth with horror she prayed that Mark was all right. Glancing around her room, she looked for her purse and realized she'd left it on the kitchen counter. There was no phone in her bedroom. She was trapped. A fist landed on her bedroom door and then she heard his voice.

"This is all your fucking fault, you bitch. If you had given me what I wanted, none of this would have happened. I'm gonna make you pay for what you've done."

The front door slammed in the distance and she hoped that Bart had left. Opening her door was one of the hardest things she'd ever had to do but Mark was out there somewhere, maybe injured. Her whole body was trembling with fear, but her brother needed her. She had to use the wall to steady herself as she walked down the hallway. When she entered the living room, she stood frozen for a moment as she stared uncomprehendingly. Mark was lying on the floor, covered in blood.

"Mark," she sobbed. She sank down next to him and ripped his shirt open. There was a bullet hole in his chest close to his heart. Justine ran to the kitchen, grabbed her cell phone from her purse and a heap of clean dish towels and hurried back to her brother, pushing 9-1-1 as she walked.

She placed three dish towels to her brother's chest and applied pressure using both hands. The cell phone was resting on her shoulder and she used her cheek to hold it there.

"9-1-1, state your emergency."

Justine spoke into the phone, all the time praying that her brother would survive. Justine disconnected once the operator told her paramedics and police were on the way.

She cried with relief when Mark opened his eyes.

"Jus, I am so sorry. I've been a terrible brother." He paused to gasp for breath and tears streamed down her face when she heard a gurgle. Blood was seeping from his mouth and the dish towels were soaked through.

"I should have taken care of you, honey." He drew in another shallow breath. "I was so messed up after they died. The drugs...You n–need to get a–away from here. Bart's...dangerous. L–Love...you." Mark's eyes stared at her and it took her a moment to realize he wasn't breathing.

She tilted his head back and breathed for him and then began pushing on his chest. It seemed like hours had passed but she knew it had only been minutes before the paramedics arrived. They used a defibrillator on her brother and placed a mask over his mouth, but nothing worked. Everything felt surreal as she watched the paramedics cover Mark's body with a sheet and call the coroner.

"Miss, are you okay?"

Justine looked up into the eyes of the concerned police officer and knew she would never be okay again.

Chapter Three

Justine entered the office of Jackson Security and walked over to her desk, waving to Garth and Derrick as they looked at her through their open office door. She'd been up all night dealing with the police, giving her statement. She was so tired all she wanted to do was curl up in bed, cry out her grief for her brother and sleep. Her energy level was nonexistent, she was running on empty, and she was in pain.

Her left eye was so swollen she could barely open it and the bruising on her cheek was so dark it was nearly black. She'd been wearing her sunglasses since she'd walked out the front door of her rental, and had no intention of taking them off while she worked, and she'd tried to cover her bruised cheek by applying makeup. It had been a painful experience, but she had persevered and hoped like hell it would be enough to hide the bruising. Even though she thought that the Jacksons would give her time off after what had happened, she had no intention of asking for it. She had no money left and she needed her next paycheck. One thing she was really glad of right at that moment was that she had her back to the two men. The last thing she needed was for them to start asking questions until she broke down. She was only hanging onto her emotions by a thin thread, and anyone being nice to her would set her off, but she had no intention of breaking down while at work.

After putting her purse away, she turned the answering machine off and booted up the computer.

"Justine, can you come in here for a bit?" Derrick called out. "I want to show you our price lists and how we do quotes."

She didn't want to go in there but she couldn't refuse. This was what she had been employed to do and she still had so much to learn. With a sigh of resignation she rose to her feet. Her head and face were throbbing and she felt herself sway slightly. Gripping the edge of her desk until the dizziness passed, she then slowly turned and walked into Derrick and Garth's office. Derrick's phone had just rung and he held up a finger without looking at her, silently asking her to wait. Garth was looking at his computer monitor and talking on the phone, too. *Thank you, God.*

Justine eased herself into a seat that was placed in front of and between the two desks. She wasn't really feeling well and being off her feet helped.

Derrick looked up and roared, "Jesus fucking Christ, I'll call you back."

He slammed the phone down and was around his desk and on his knees in front of her within the blink of an eye. When he reached up for her sunglasses she leaned back away from him.

"Don't move," he said in a deep, commanding voice, and even though she was still in a great deal of pain, the tone and the timbre of his voice caused her to shiver with sexual awareness. But it also made her freeze into compliance.

What is up with that?

Derrick removed her sunglasses and gasped. "Who did this to you?"

"Fuck," Garth yelled and hurried to her side. He reached out to touch her face but drew back when she flinched. "I would never hurt you, Justine. What the hell happened to you?"

She drew a shaky breath and blinked, trying to control the tears that were forming at the back of her eyes. She opened her mouth to begin explaining, but before she could, another masculine voice drew the Jackson brothers' attention.

"What the hell is wrong with you?" Matt asked angrily. "You nearly ruptured my fucking eardrum. My ear is still fucking ringing."

Justine didn't dare look at Matt. It was bad enough that her bosses hadn't taken their eyes off of her, but then he was standing behind Derrick and she slowly met his gaze.

"Shit. Who the hell hit you?" She flinched since it seemed like his anger was now directed at her.

"No one in this office would ever hurt someone weaker than they are, Justine." Derrick cupped her chin. "Please don't be scared of us. We're worried about you, honey. Now tell me who hurt you."

His voice was so deep and demanding she didn't stand a chance. Justine found herself telling the three men about last night and wondered why she all of a sudden felt so numb. By the time she had finished explaining, the pounding in her head had intensified and she felt physically sick. She was swaying in her seat, cold to the bone and shaking like a leaf.

"Whoa." Derrick gripped her shoulders to keep her from falling and she was truly grateful, because she felt like she could have fallen to the floor like a puddle of melted ice. "Garth, call Nate Charleston I want her checked over."

"Have you seen a doctor, baby?"

It took her a moment to register that Garth was talking to her. The paramedics who had taken Mark's body away had given her a cursory medical exam, had told her nothing was broken, then advised her to put ice on her eye and cheek and to get some rest. That hadn't been possible. Justine had spent hours going over what had happened with the police and coroner, and by the time they had left, all she wanted to do was shower and fall into bed. She'd showered but the rest had been pushed aside because she'd had to get to work.

She shook her head when she remembered she hadn't answered Garth and groaned because the movement only increased the pain in her cheek, eyes, and head, and made the dizziness worse. She reached up to clutch her head, but her arm felt so damn heavy she could barely lift it. Her vision became blurry and began to diminish. The coffee she'd had that morning roiled in her stomach and she was thankful she hadn't eaten anything. Her stomach heaved and she knew she was going to be ill. She opened her mouth to warn them but lost the contents of her stomach instead, and then she fainted for the first time in her life.

* * * *

"Fuck. Get her upstairs to our apartment," Garth said and pulled his cell phone from his pocket and began talking to Dr. Nathan Charleston. Derrick had never been so glad in his life that Nate's clinic was only two buildings from theirs and hoped that their friend would hurry.

Derrick gently lifted Justine into his arms and headed for the door. "Matt can you stay down here and direct Nate up to our rooms when he arrives?"

"Sure, I'll clean up, too."

"Thank you." Derrick didn't spare his friend and employee another glance but hurried out of the office and to the locked door at the back of the building. Garth used his thumbprint to open the door and then held it so he could carry Justine through. He rushed up the stairs to the top floor, which had been converted into a large apartment, and stepped aside so Garth could open that door, too.

Derrick carried Justine straight to the large bathroom and with his brother's help, removed her soiled clothes, handed her over to Garth, turned the shower on and adjusted the temperature. Once he, too, had stripped down, he took Justine back and stepped into the running water. He'd hoped the water would help revive her, but she didn't even stir and he was becoming very worried.

"Garth, I'm going to need your help in here."

Garth removed his clothes and got into the shower. Between the two of them, they washed Justine's hair and body and themselves. Garth got out first, dried off and hurried out to the bedrooms to get some clothes. They dried her off and dressed her in one of Derrick's

T-shirts. Garth shifted her in his arms and out to the bedroom while Derrick dried and dressed in clean clothes.

Derrick pulled the covers up over Justine just as the doorbell to their apartment rang. Garth hurried out to let Nate in.

"What's the problem? Who is the woman?" Dr. Nate Charleston walked toward the bed.

Derrick explained and then waited with bated breath as Nate examined Justine. He took her blood pressure, listened to her heart, and examined her swollen black eye and cheek.

"I don't think there is anything seriously wrong with her, apart from the swollen eye and bruised cheek. Do you know if she has eaten anything today?"

"No clue," Garth answered.

"You said she spent hours talking to the cops. Maybe she didn't have any sleep, and if she hasn't eaten, she would be feeling pretty drained." Nate sat on the edge of the bed and turned toward Garth. "I'd say she is probably suffering shock, too. She found her brother on the living room floor with a hole in his chest and she was there when he passed away. Considering everything she's just been through, she must be totally exhausted. Let her sleep for a couple of hours and if she doesn't wake up, call me. I have to get back to the clinic. I have patients to see."

"Thanks, Nate." Garth walked Nate to the door. Once their doctor friend had left, Derrick pulled a chair from near the wall to close to the bed and sat down. Garth did the same.

"God, she's beautiful," Garth whispered. "I have never seen such a gorgeous woman."

"Yeah, you have," Derrick replied. "You're just drawn to her the same way I am."

"I'm glad it's not just me. I've been hard since the moment she walked into the office."

"Me, too," Derrick sighed. "She is naturally so damn submissive and I don't think she has a clue."

"There's more of a story with her brother than she's told us."

"Yeah, I got that from her phone conversation with the asshole and his fucking friend yesterday."

"Shit." Garth looked at him. "She could still be in danger."

"Fuck. I'd forgotten about that bastard. I wonder if the cops have picked him up yet?"

"Only one way to find out." Garth rose to his feet, pulling his cell from his pocket, and walked toward the bedroom door. "I'll see what I can find out. Gary Wade may be able to fill us in, and if he isn't aware of her situation, he can do some digging."

Derrick nodded and felt a little of the tension ease away. He and Garth were Dominants and members of Club of Dominance. They were friends with a lot of the other Doms and often hung out with their friends at the club. Gary Wade was also a detective and a Dom. If he couldn't tell them anything, then no one could.

Justine moaned and he pushed to his feet and rushed over to the bed. He hated that she was in pain and sick. He wanted to wrap her up in his arms and hold her tight, but she had only just met him and his brother, so if they wanted a relationship with her, they were going to have to take things slow. He just hoped that what had happened to her didn't have her running scared from them.

Derrick sat on the side of the bed near her hip, reached up, and gently brushed the hair away from her face. She sighed and then her eyelids lifted. She blinked a few times and then stared at him with a frown.

"How are you feeling, Justine?"

"What happened?" Her frown intensified and then memory must have returned, because her face went bright pink. "Oh shit. Did I throw up on you?"

"Don't worry about that, baby. What's a little vomit between friends?"

"Oh God. I'm sorry."

"Hey don't worry about it, sweetie. Are you feeling any better?"

"Yes." She looked about the room. "Where am I?"

"You're in our upstairs apartment. We called our doctor friend to come and check you over."

"Thank you, but I'm fine."

"No, you're fucking not," Garth said as he walked into the room. "Your eye is almost swollen shut and your cheek is terribly bruised. When was the last time you ate?"

"Um…"

"That's what I thought," Garth snapped. Derrick frowned at Garth, trying to get him to back off, but he knew his brother wasn't about to. They were both very attracted to Justine, and now that she worked for them, she also came under their protection.

Justine pushed the covers down, her intention to get out of bed clear, but she gasped when she saw the cotton material covering her chest. She lifted the quilt and peered down at her body.

"You were covered in vomit, Justine. We had to clean you up before putting you to bed."

She frowned and blushed and then pulled the covers back up and nodded at Derrick.

"I've put your clothes in the washing machine." Garth sighed and scrubbed a hand over his face. "You can have them back after they've been through the dryer."

"Thank you."

Garth nodded. "I'm going to fix you something to eat. How's your stomach?"

"Fine."

Garth had turned away, obviously heading for the kitchen, but he spun back. "You'd say that even if you weren't fine. Wouldn't you, Justine?"

Derrick watched his brother stalk toward the bed, anger radiating out of every pore. He stepped in front of Garth, halting his brother's progress and spoke low enough that Justine wouldn't hear him.

"Not yet, brother. She's not ready."

Garth let out a frustrated sigh and spun back around and left the room without a backward glance. Derrick sat on the side of the bed and watched her intently. He wanted some honesty from Justine and he wasn't going to put up with any lies.

"How much pain are you in?"

She met his gaze, pulled her lips in tight and looked away. He reached over and gently gripped her chin so she couldn't glance away again.

"Fine," she snapped. "My eye and cheek are throbbing like a bitch. I have a headache, and I am so damn tired I can barely think straight."

"Good..."

"Good?" she screeched. "You think it's good that I feel like shit?"

Her cheeks flushed with her fit of pique and her eyes gleamed with an inner fire. He was seeing a bit of the real Justine Downey and couldn't wait until he had all of her. Derrick had no intention of letting her get away from him. Not when he'd just found the woman who could be "the one" for them.

"Quiet," he said in his Dom voice and was pleased when she closed her mouth and glared at him.

"I'm not happy that you are in pain and aren't feeling well, baby. I'm happy that you were finally honest with me." He caressed her cheek with his thumb and then withdrew his hand from her face. "After you've eaten, I'll give you some pain killers and you can take another nap."

"No, I need to get dressed and get back to work. You're not paying me to stay in bed all day."

"Enough," Garth said as he walked into the bedroom, carrying a tray. "You will be taking the rest of the day off. If I had my way, you would take the next two weeks to recuperate."

"I can't do that. I need to work," Justine snapped and folded her arms over her chest.

"We'll discuss it later." Garth placed the tray over her lap. "For now you need to eat and rest."

Derrick was pleased that Garth hadn't brought Justine anything too heavy to eat. The soup and toast should be okay for her to keep down. They sat silently and watched her eat and although he could tell she was a little uncomfortable at their silent vigil, he wasn't about to leave. He needed to know that she was cared for and he wasn't going to let her get away without finishing everything Garth had prepared for her. By the time she'd finished, her eyelids were drooping again so he removed the tray and placed it on the bedside table. He went to the bathroom, shook out two painkillers from the bottle, and filled a glass with water, and when he was back at her bedside, he handed her the medicine and watched as she swallowed them.

"Close your eyes and rest, Justine. Your body needs sleep to recuperate." Derrick was pleased when she moved down the bed with her head once more on the pillow. It wasn't long before her breathing evened out.

"Gary called me while I was getting Justine's food." Garth ran a hand through his hair. He only ever did that if he was really worried about something. "That bastard Bart Devrees is still at large. I don't want her out of our sight until he's caught. That fucker was going to rape her and when her brother found him and tried to kick him out, he killed him. He's dangerous."

"Do the police have any leads? Do they have any idea where he may have gone?"

"No, he doesn't have a rap sheet. I'd say he's been damn lucky to avoid the cops. A leopard doesn't change its spots overnight. I have a bad feeling about this dude."

"Yeah, me, too." Derrick sighed. "I don't want her going back home."

"Me either, but how the hell are we going to keep her here or get her to come to the house with us? She's going to baulk if we suggest she should stay with us."

"Maybe, but her safety is more important than her anger. We'll just have to tell her the truth. We can't keep this from her, Garth. She needs to be aware of the danger she's in."

"You really think this fucker Bart is going to come back for her?"

"I'd bet my life on it."

Chapter Four

"What do you mean I can't go home? The police have finished doing whatever they needed to. One of the policemen called me to tell me it was okay to go back." Justine frowned at her new bosses. She had spent the entire day in bed and felt much better. Although she'd never admit it to them, the thought of going home made her feel ill. She still hadn't cleaned up the blood from the floor and she was so damn scared Bart would come back for her. He had a key so he would have no problem getting into the house, and there was no way she could afford to have all the locks changed. If she was able to sleep, she may not hear him come in and would be a sitting duck.

"Justine, I know you aren't stupid. There is blood all over the place and I'm sure you don't want to have to deal with that." When Derrick reached for her hand, she felt all the blood drain from her face and she shivered. He pulled her into his arms and held her close.

Justine wanted to stay where she was and soak up his strength and comfort, but she had learned to depend on no one, and if she gave in, she was scared that she would enjoy letting them take control and wouldn't be able to stand on her own two feet again. When she pushed against his chest, he released her. She took a deep, shaky breath and released it slowly.

"Did the officer also tell you they haven't found Bart?" Garth asked.

"Yes."

"Goddamn it, Justine," Garth said angrily. "What the hell are you thinking? You know damn well that he could come after you. Do you know how to protect yourself against someone like that? He killed you brother, damn it. He shot him in cold blood."

Justine turned her back on the two men. She'd been trying to hold it together, but tears leaked out of her eyes and ran down her face. Although she hadn't liked what her brother had become, she'd still loved him and now she would never see him again. Her chest was tight with pain, a knot of grief so big she didn't think she could contain it anymore. The first sob caught her by surprise, and even though she tried to hold it in, she couldn't.

Sinking to her knees as pain overwhelmed her, she wrapped her arms around her waist and gave in. Justine cried and cried and cried. She so was scared that she would never be able to stop that she was barely aware of arms wrapping around her and lifting her up. Finally the pain in her chest eased slightly and her tears began to dry up. An occasional hiccup wracked her body and she became aware of the warmth wrapped around her and the hard thighs beneath her ass. Her fingers were twisted in the material of a shirt and she unwound them and let the fabric go. She had been clutching it like it was her only lifeline, and at that moment it had been.

She wiped her face and sniffed but kept her forehead pressed against the warm, hard chest it was resting on. She needed a tissue in the worst way, but she was embarrassed over her breakdown and didn't want to see their faces.

When a wad of clean tissues was placed into her hand, she nodded gratefully and blew her nose. A large, warm hand was caressing up and down her back and another was rubbing over her shoulder and down her arm. Neither of the men said anything and for that she was thankful. She didn't want to hear their pity, because it would probably set her off again. Taking a deep shuddering breath, she finally gathered her courage and lifted her head. What she saw in their eyes as she connected with each of their gazes made her fall a little in love with them. There was no pity, only concern, and it was all for her. No one besides her parents had ever worried about her. Not even her brother. For the first time since she was eleven years old, she was being held and didn't want to let go.

Without any conscious thought, she reached up and grabbed two handfuls of Derrick's hair, pulled his head down toward hers, and placed her lips on his. She brushed them back and forth over his and then licked over his lower lip. Derrick's passionate growl pushed her excitement higher and then she was moaning into his mouth as he took over the kiss.

His tongue pushed in and slid along hers. She gripped his hair tighter and moaned when he tangled his tongue around hers and pulled it into his mouth. He suckled on her, and her desire to have him, *them*, burned her from the inside out. Justine had never felt so alive, so wanted or needed. She wanted the Jackson brothers to strip her naked and fuck her until she screamed, to let her know that she was alive.

Derrick lifted her without breaking their kiss. He lowered her feet to the floor and she felt his hands on the buttons of her newly washed shirt. She released his hair and ran her hands over his shoulders and down his chest. Her clit pulsed and filled with need and her pussy clenched, soaking the crotch of her panties. His mouth slid from her lips and across her uninjured cheek and then he nipped at her earlobe and kissed and licked his way down the side of her neck.

Large hands pushed the shirt from her shoulders and down her arms. Another set of hands pulled the material over her hands and she shivered as the cool air caressed her skin. The catch on her bra was released and she groaned when her breasts were cupped from behind and lifted as if in offering.

"Are you sure you want this, Justine?" Garth asked. "We don't want you thinking this has anything to do with your job."

"No. I–I mean yes. I want this. I know this has n–nothing to do with w–work."

"Be very sure, darlin'. I don't want you thinking we took advantage of you."

"I need this," she gasped. "I–I need your hands and mouths on me, to make me feel a–alive. Please."

Derrick had been holding off until she'd answered Garth, but when the last word left her mouth, he then took his brother's offering and laved his tongue around the areola and over the tip of her nipple and then suckled on her strongly. She shook with arousal and gasped for air. Her whole body was on fire and she didn't know how to put it out. The hands holding her breasts up released her aching globes and caressed down her sides and then moved around to the front of her slacks. They tugged the snaps open and then the pants were being pushed down over her hips with her panties.

Derrick released her nipple with a wet pop and then he scooped her up in his arms and placed her in the middle of the bed. When her gaze met his, the heat in his eyes only made her fire burn hotter, brighter. She reached out her arms in silent invitation and then watched as his fingers worked the buttons on his shirt and he pulled it from his body. Justine gasped in awe, absolutely floored at the beauty of his physique. His shoulders were wide and his chest and upper arms were thick with muscle. Power radiated from him as his sinew and tendons rippled each time he moved. Movement off to the side caught her attention and she bit her lip to keep a groan of desire from escaping

Garth was even more brawny than Derrick. His lightly tanned skin gleamed in the waning afternoon light and she wanted nothing more than to run her hands all over their bodies and indulge in the feel of their skin and muscle beneath her hands. Garth kept her gaze pinned with his as he walked toward her and climbed onto the bed next to her. There was heat in his eyes, but she could see other emotions beneath that hunger. She didn't want to know what he was thinking. All she wanted to do was feel. He leaned over her and covered her lips with his.

Garth kissed differently than Derrick. Derrick coaxed and seduced where Garth almost demanded a response. His tongue thrust in between her lips and he explored every inch of her interior. By the time he brought his tongue back to dance with hers, she was so breathless she was scared she would pass out. He lifted his head, cupped a breast with his hand and then he sucked a nipple into his mouth. Justine cried out as sparks of lust shot from her breast straight down to her pussy, causing her internal walls to clench and more of her juices leaked out.

"I can smell your musk, baby." Derrick's voice was raspy with hunger and she lifted her head to look at him and found him sitting back on his heels between her splayed thighs. God, she'd been so wrapped up in Garth, she hadn't even felt Derrick get on the bed with her. "I want to taste you, Justine."

Justine whimpered, her head flopped back onto the pillow and her eyes closed. Derrick shifted on the mattress and then she felt his hot breath fanning over her pussy. She couldn't stop from pushing her hips up, begging him without words to place his mouth on her.

A slap landed on her thigh, and if Garth hadn't quickly placed his hand in the center of her chest, she would have bolted upright. "What the hell was that for?" Justine asked, lifting her head to glare at Derrick. But then she wiggled her hips as the warmth blossoming on her thigh close to her vagina spread up to her cunt and more juices oozed out.

"You liked that bit of pain, didn't you, baby?"

Justine shook her head but couldn't keep looking into his eyes.

"Don't lie, Justine," Garth said after releasing her nipple. "We are trained to know when a sub likes a bite of pain."

Sub? Does he mean what I think he means?

"We are Doms, baby. Do you know what a Dom is?" Derrick asked in that deep voice that sent shivers traversing up and down her spine.

"I–I…"

"We like to be in control in the bedroom, Justine. In fact we like to control everything when it comes to sex. Have you ever been to a

BDSM club, honey?" Garth moved his palm from the middle of her chest and caressed down her stomach and then back up again. Not getting close to where she ached for his touch.

"No," she answered. *Was that my voice sounding so breathy? What is happening to me? Why does it turn me on to know that these two men are Dominants?* Her insides were so hot she thought she just may combust. The ache inside was so intense it was overwhelming. In all her twenty-three years she had never experienced such strong reactions before and had no idea how to handle what she was feeling.

"You are a natural submissive, Justine." Garth's fingers caressed down her belly again and tickled through the hair at the top of her mound. She held her breath, hoping he would touch lower. "You have a need to be controlled, to be dominated in bed, and we would love to show you how much pleasure we can bring you. One night soon, we want to take you to the club, but right now we intend to give you more pleasure than you've ever experienced before."

Justine was already getting more pleasure than she'd previously experienced and didn't know if she could take much more. She wanted to feel them making love to her and she wanted it now, but had no idea how to go about asking for what she needed.

She'd only ever had one lover and that had been a total bust. After that, she'd decided that maybe sex wasn't all it was made out to be and focused on getting her business management degree instead.

The yearning deep inside to let go and just give herself over to them was such a strong craving she was almost shaking with it, but she had learned to be cautious and wasn't about to let them take her over. If she did come to depend on them and things didn't work out, she would be back to square one and she didn't want to have to start all over again to build those protective walls up to keep her heart safe from more pain.

"What are you thinking about, baby?" Derrick's hands skimmed up her thighs, getting closer and closer to her throbbing pussy. It took all her concentration not to arch her hips up and silently beg for his touch and to answer his question.

"It doesn't matter."

"Now, that's where you're wrong, darlin'." Garth kissed her shoulder and then grasped her chin in his hand. "Everything about you matters, but I can see you don't trust us enough to open up to us yet, but you will in time."

Justine wasn't so sure about that. It was hard for her to trust and she didn't know if she would ever be able to have faith in anyone enough to open up and lay her heart bare. Garth released her chin, leaned over, and took her mouth. Her libido, which had begun to ease, flamed back to life as he devoured her. His tongue slid along hers and his masculine flavor exploded on her taste buds. She'd never felt anything like this and didn't think she ever would again.

Derrick shifted on the mattress and then he pushed her thighs further apart. When she felt his warm breath on the curls of her mound, she couldn't prevent herself from arching up into him. She needed him to touch her aching pussy before she went out of her mind with lust. Garth released her mouth and then he kissed his way down to her chest. His wet heat enveloped her nipple, sending zings of electrical sparks to her pussy and then she cried out as Derrick's tongue licked through her dew-covered folds, eliciting a need so great, for a moment she couldn't draw another breath.

Justine finally inhaled and then she sobbed when Derrick's tongue laved over her engorged, aching clit. The rapture she experienced brought another cry to her lips. Garth released her nipple with a wet-sounding plop, and then he grasped both arms in his hands and held them to the mattress beside her head. She looked up into his beautiful eyes and gasped at the hungry heat she saw in them, but that wasn't all she saw. There was a determination in his gaze that caused her to shiver.

"Look at you," Garth rasped. "You're so fucking sexy and beautiful. Your face is flushed and you're writhing with need. My cock is aching to be in your pussy, baby."

Justine knew he was right about her not being still. The harder she tried to keep from moving, the more she wriggled with desire. With her hands pinned on either side of her head, she felt so controlled and it turned her on.

Derrick sucked her clit into his mouth and she cried out at the bliss of such exquisite torture. She wanted his cock in her aching cunt and arched up into his mouth, but then he moved his big hands from her inner thighs and placed one on her lower belly just above her pubis, while the other hand, she found out a second later, was between her splayed legs. The tip of a finger rimmed around her pussy hole and only enhanced the ecstasy he was bestowing on her. He released her clit and moved his head back down, sliding his tongue between the lips of her sex as he slurped up all her cream.

"You taste so fucking good, darlin', I can't wait to get my cock in this tight little pussy."

Justine couldn't believe the way they talked dirty to her, but she also couldn't believe how that only seemed to turn her on more. Before she could analyze the way they made her feel connected to them, Derrick was pushing a finger into her pussy. She turned her head toward her left arm and placed her mouth on her bicep to muffle the sounds coming from her mouth. Even to her own ears, she sounded like an animal in heat, and that scared the absolute crap out of her.

Garth tugged on her hair and she moved her head away from her arm as he demanded, "Don't you dare try to hide from us, Justine. We want to hear every sound you make and see the pleasure on your face."

"Oh God," she sobbed when Derrick added another finger to her pussy and moved his tongue more rapidly over her clit. Warmth permeated her body from the inside out. Her womb felt heavy and achy and her internal muscles wouldn't stop their incessant clenching. The tension in her muscles grew and grew until she was scared she would break apart and there was nothing she could do to stop the prodigious sensations. Not that she really wanted to. It was just that what she was experiencing was so phenomenal that she was amazed by her own body's uninhibited responses.

Tingles of heat swept out and over her, making her legs tremble and her toes curl. And then she was flying. Sparks of electrical light flashed before her eyes, and she screamed as rapture assailed her. Blackness crept around the edge of her vision as her pussy clamped and released, clutched and let go, over and over again. And just as the nirvana began to wane Derrick did something inside her that sent her up and over the precipice once more. She opened her mouth on a silent scream and felt cream expel from her pussy in a big gush as her whole body quaked. When the final wave of joy faded, the only sound she could hear was that of three adults breathing heavily. Her eyelids were closed and she couldn't even remember shutting them.

When Derrick removed his fingers from her pussy, she whimpered as an aftershock wracked her body and her sensitive flesh quivered. She became aware of hands running over her arms and legs in a soothing manner and she sighed with satiation. When she opened her eyes, Derrick was sitting up between her legs and Garth was lying on his side with his head resting on his hand.

"You're beautiful when you come, darlin'," Derrick said in a deep, hoarse voice. "We can't wait to make love with you, but now isn't the time." He patted her leg and then got off the bed. She looked his delectably cut body over and licked her lips. She couldn't believe that her just-sated lust began to simmer back to life when her eyes snagged on the large bulge beneath his jeans. From what she could see, the man wasn't lacking in the penis department. If anything, he had been very blessed and she was a little nervous about fitting something that big inside her pussy.

Garth spoke, drawing her attention, and she was glad that Derrick hadn't seen where she had been looking. "Why don't you get cleaned up and come on out to the living room." Garth rolled off the bed and then headed toward the door. "We have a few things we need to discuss with you."

Justine watched with confusion as they left. She wasn't sure she wanted to face them after what she had just let them do to her. She was embarrassed over her behavior of practically jumping on Derrick. *God, what have I done? They are my employers.* But she remembered Garth saying that what they had done didn't have anything to do with her job. She was going to have to brazen it out when she met them face to face again. But then confusion made her frown. What man gave a woman pleasure without taking his own? In fact, what man gave a woman any pleasure at all? From her one and only experience, a man's needs were the only thing that mattered and once he had climaxed then everything was finished. But the two men had left the room with huge hard-ons.

Derrick and Garth Jackson were a conundrum she didn't think she would ever be able to figure out.

Chapter Five

"She's going to be embarrassed about what happened." Garth took a sip of coffee and stared at the door to the hallway across the room. Justine had had plenty of time to shower and get dressed, but he and Derrick were still waiting for her to show her face.

"Yeah." Derrick stared into his mug. "We can't let her go back to her rental. Her life is still in danger, but I don't know if she'll agree to come home with us."

"She can always stay here if she baulks about coming with us. There is always someone on duty monitoring things in the control room. She'd be just as safe here as she would be at our home."

"I don't want to let her out of our sight." Derrick scrubbed a hand over his face. "God, she is so perfect for us. I've never seen a more responsive sub in my life."

"I know. All the women we've played with over the years don't even compare. After being with Justine, I can't even remember them. That woman has so much love to give and has such a compassionate nature. We could have everything with her. But it's going to take time to get her to trust us and get through those walls she built up."

"She trusts us with her body."

"That's not enough, Derrick. I want her to trust us with her heart and soul, too."

"I know, but we've only just met, Garth. We can't go rushing in like a bull in a china shop. She'll just fortify those walls around her heart if we do."

Garth was about to respond but closed his mouth when he heard a rustle from the hallway. It seemed that Justine had finally found the courage to face them. When she entered the living room, she looked cool and calm, but he knew better. Her shoulders were raised up with tension and her hands were clenched into little fists. He wanted to rush over to her and pull her into his arms and reassure her that everything would be all right, but he held off. He wanted to see how she would handle things. She met his eyes for a moment and then glanced toward Derrick. Her eyes skittered away and she looked around the room like she was trying to find something.

Derrick stood and headed toward the kitchen. "Take a seat darlin'. I'll get you some coffee."

Justine's shoulders slumped and then she walked over to the other armchair. It seemed their little sub was going to keep her distance. Derrick came back and handed her a mug and took his seat again. She kept her eyes lowered and took a sip from her cup and then wrapped her other hand around it. It looked like it was up to him and Derrick to begin talking.

"Justine, I contacted a detective friend of mine while you were sleeping earlier and asked if the police have picked up this asshole, Bart. They haven't been able to find him, baby. I don't like the idea of you going back home where you'll be all alone. That fucker was going to rape you, Justine. You need to come home with us so we can protect you. We served our country in the Marines for nearly eight years and have kept up our physical fitness by doing martial arts. We have all the necessary skills to keep you safe. "

"Okay, thank you."

Her answer was so unexpected Garth was speechless.

"Can I ask you something?" Justine asked.

"You can ask us anything you like, baby." Garth relaxed into his seat, some of his tension draining away, glad that she was finally willing to talk to them.

"Why didn't either of you want to have sex with me?"

Derrick shifted on the sofa so he was facing Justine more directly. "We did want to make love with you, darlin', don't ever think that we don't, but we weren't about to take advantage of you when you were in such a fragile state. We shouldn't have even done what we did, since you were so upset, but we just couldn't seem to help ourselves."

Garth leaned forward resting his arms on his knees. "You are still grieving, Justine. We would have been assholes to benefit from that. When we make love to you we don't want you to have any reason to regret it. We already know you are embarrassed about what happened between us, not that you have any reason to be ashamed, baby. You needed the reaffirmation of being alive after losing a loved one.

"Derrick and I are as attracted to you as you are to us and it took every bit of our self-control to not strip down and love you. But that wouldn't have been fair to you, baby. Firstly, you are injured and still in pain. There was no way we were going to take a chance and cause you more hurt. Secondly, when we make love to you, we want it to mean something to you."

Garth watched the expressions flit across her face. He knew she didn't know what he meant and that was okay, since it was too early in the scheme of things for her to know what he or his brother wanted from her. Justine needed more time to get to know them and to learn to trust her own instincts as well as her heart. He'd already figured out she trusted them, if only a little bit. She never would have allowed them to touch her if she didn't have any belief in their reliability.

She took a deep breath and then looked at him again. "I need to go home and get some of my things."

"That's not a good idea, darlin'," Derrick said. "Bart could be lying in wait for you. Why don't you give me the key to your place and I'll pack a bag for you?"

"Okay." Justine rose to her feet and so did Garth. "I need to get my purse."

"I have a better idea." Garth walked over to her side and took her hand in his. "Derrick and I will take you home and I'll send Matt and Luke to your place. Their shift finishes in about five minutes. I'm sure they won't mind helping out. I'll order some pizzas as a thank you and we can watch a movie while we eat. I don't want you anywhere near that place, Justine. If Bart is watching, he isn't going to sit back and do nothing. That man wants you bad and I don't think he's going to stop until he gets what he wants. But we aren't about to let him get anywhere near you. Okay?"

"Okay." Justine shivered and Garth cursed his tactlessness. The last thing he wanted to do was frighten her, but she needed to be aware that Bart was a serious threat. If he had his way, Justine would never be out of his sight ever again. He and Derrick had lost their eldest cousin, Louise, years ago to someone just like Bart. If they hadn't been in the Middle East at the time serving their country they would have hunted that fucker down and taken him out. Ever since then they had vowed to somehow set up a business to protect those weaker than they were. Derrick had come up with the security company business just before their time in the Marines was served. It had taken a lot of hard work and planning, and thanks to Matt and Luke, between the four of them they had just enough cash to start their company. And now, years down the track, they had a very lucrative business and had stopped a lot of people getting hurt.

Derrick had taken Justine back to the reception area to get her purse and Garth had headed toward the control room to intercept Matt and Luke, but as soon as he reached the door, they both walked out.

"Did you inform the others about the situation with Justine?" Garth asked.

"We did," Luke replied. "Jayden and Josh will be on the lookout for anyone hanging around. Do you think this fucker knows where she is?"

"Yeah." Garth sighed with frustration. "She called her brother yesterday with the office phone number and address in case of an emergency, and the asshole called her not an hour later. He's going to be watching for her at her house and when she doesn't turn up there he will come here."

"Do we have a description of this asshole?" Matt asked.

"We should by now." Garth turned and headed down the hall toward the office, his friends following behind. He paused near the reception desk when Derrick handed over Justine's house keys and rattled off her address. He nodded and then waved Matt and Luke into the office.

"I want you guys to go to her house and pack her clothes, enough to last a few weeks." Garth walked over to the fax machine and retrieved the printout. The description lacked any picture. He read through the asshole's statistics and knew it would be hard to know if he or anyone else came face to face with Bart. The first thing he wanted to do tonight was see if Luke could create an artist's depiction of Bart with Justine's help. Hopefully by the end of the night Garth would be able to hand over a sketch to Gary Wade. It would go a long way in helping the law find the fucker who had tried to rape Justine. He wouldn't be able to rest until the bastard was behind bars for murder and attempted rape.

Garth went to the photocopy machine and ran off ten copies of Bart's description and handed them over to Matt before turning to Luke. "We'll order some pizza for dinner. I would really appreciate it if you could work with Justine and get a sketch of this asshole."

"Sure," Luke said. "Give us about two hours. I'll need to get home for my charcoal and pad."

"No problem. See you soon."

Garth followed them out into the reception area where Justine and Derrick were waiting. Although Justine had spent a lot of the day sleeping, she was still too pale and tired looking. From now on he was going to make sure she rested as much as possible and ate regularly. Since she'd been the one working to earn the money as well as keeping house and cooking all the meals, he doubted that she'd had a spare minute to herself. Garth wondered what had motivated her brother to be such a lazy asshole. As far as he and Derrick were concerned, women should be taken care of, not taken advantage of.

"Are you ready to go?"

"Yes." Justine headed for the door.

"Our truck is out the back, baby. Let me lock up and I'll meet you at the back door." Garth locked up quickly and hurried after them. He wanted Justine in between him and Derrick in case that fucker Bart was watching and decided to take a pot shot at her. If Bart wanted Justine, he'd have to go through Derrick and Garth first.

They paused once they reached the back door of the office while Derrick peeked his head out and scanned the area before giving him the all clear signal. Then Derrick reached back for Justine's hand and led her out. Garth stayed close to her back and kept his eyes peeled and his hand on the gun in his waistband. He'd slid the pistol into his jeans before leaving the office just in case. He watched the shadows, and even though he couldn't see anyone, he didn't relax until she was in the front seat of the truck between him and Derrick.

Derrick started the truck and pulled out of the rear parking lot. Justine sat quietly between them and stared out the windshield but he could see and feel the tension emanating from her. He needed to get her to relax and let those walls down, and right now the only way he could think to do that was to get her talking.

"What do you like on your pizza, Justine?"

She turned to face him. "Anything but anchovies."

"Well, that's good, you're easy to please."

Derrick seemed to take the silence that followed as a cue to interject. "Why did you let your brother treat you like shit?"

Garth mentally cursed Derrick's bluntness. Usually he was the tactless one, not his brother. He just hoped Derrick's candor didn't make Justine angry. His sibling was trying to understand how Justine's mind worked, and if he didn't want to know the same thing, he would have stepped in and redirected the conversation.

"Mark was all I had," Justine said quietly.

"Where are your parents?" Garth asked the question this time.

"They died in the terrorist attack on the Twin Towers in New York on 9/11. They both worked for the same investment firm in the

North Tower of the World Trade Center. They…didn't make it through the attacks. Their offices were right above where the first plane hit."

"Shit, you were only a kid," Derrick said. "Didn't you have any relatives to help you out?"

"Not that I'm aware of. Neither of my parents had siblings, and their parents had already passed away before Mark and I were born."

"So what happened? How did you end up in Oregon?"

Justine sighed as if reluctant to go into depth, but Garth wanted to hear it all.

"Mark and I were put into foster care but no one would take the both of us in."

Justine went on to explain how they had been separated and she hadn't heard from her brother until just before she turned eighteen.

He understood how adrift they both must have felt, but when Mark had turned eighteen and left the foster care system, his priority should have been looking for his sister and then making damn sure she was taken care of. The more he learned about her brother, the more he disliked him, but he wouldn't have wished him dead.

Derrick turned into their drive and then parked in the garage. He glanced toward Garth over Justine's head and he could see the ire in Derrick's eyes and the way his jaw was clenched tight.

"Okay, let's get inside and we'll show you around."

They showed her around the house and then led her to the master bedroom. "This will be your room while you're here." Garth swept out a hand to direct her further into the room.

"But this is the main bedroom. Doesn't one of you sleep here?" Justine frowned.

"No." Derrick leaned just inside the door against the wall. "Our bedrooms are on either side of this one. We want to be able to protect you, Justine. This way no one can come down the hall without either of us hearing them. They'd have to pass our bedroom doors before they got to yours."

"Are you sure you want me to have this room?"

"Yes, baby. Now don't argue, you won't change our minds," Garth said in a firm voice, letting a bit of his inner Dom out.

"Okay." Justine sighed. "Thank you."

"Come on out to the kitchen." Derrick pushed off from the wall and held a hand out to her. "You can help me start of pot of coffee. That way you'll know where everything is."

Justine took Derrick's hand and followed him out. Garth walked behind her and couldn't stop himself from watching the graceful sway of her hips.

An hour later Garth heard Matt and Luke pull up outside. He left Derrick and Justine where they were, sitting on the sofa, snuggled up together, watching a movie, and went to the door. He stepped out onto the porch and closed the front door behind him. When he saw the angry expressions on Matt's and Luke's faces, he knew something was wrong.

The men got out of their truck and Matt got a small bag from the back seat.

"Is that all you got? Where are the rest of Justine's things?"

"That asshole has been back to the house." The muscle in Luke's clenched jaw jumped. "He trashed the whole place. Nearly everything she owns has been destroyed. The fucker cut up all her clothes and ruined the furniture. I called Gary Wade. He came and brought some of his men over to check it out. But he said that taking fingerprints probably wouldn't help much and would be a waste of time, because Bart had been living in that house for nearly five years and his prints were bound to be all over the place. He was still getting one of the forensic officers to bring a kit over, though."

"Fuck!" Garth turned toward the door and stared at it, picturing Justine cuddled up on the lounge with his brother. She was safe and sound, thank God. He felt sick to his stomach when he realized what she could have found if they had let her go back home. "If he can't do anything, then what is the point of calling his colleagues in at all?"

Luke shrugged. "He was taking photos for evidence, and if they find this bastard and can prove he did in fact destroy Justine's things, then he can be arrested for willful damage, which will add to his murder and attempted rape charge. Gary wants to be able to put this asshole away for a long time."

"You're going to have to tell her, Garth," Matt said as he followed Garth to the front door. "She's going to know something's up since we could only salvage a few of her undamaged clothes."

"Shit." Garth paused with one hand on the doorknob and scrubbed the other over his face in frustration. Matt was right. He wouldn't be able to hide anything from her. Justine was smart and would know right away that something was wrong. Well, there wasn't much he could do about it and the more he thought about trying to hide what had happened from her, the guiltier he felt. She had a right to know what went down. The more informed she was, the more vigilant she would be. The thought of that fucker getting to her and hurting her physically made him feel ill, but he and Derrick would do everything within their power to protect her.

"You're right, she needs to know."

"We'll help you keep her safe, man." Luke thumped him on the shoulder. "Everyone at Jackson Security and our BDSM friends will help, too."

"Yeah, I know. God, I feel so fucking useless right now."

"Hey," Matt said, "you're doing everything you can under the circumstances. Just make sure that she is never left alone."

"Easier said than done, man." Garth turned the knob but didn't push the door open. "That woman has been a pillar of strength, taking care of everyone else around her. How the hell are we going to convince her to put herself in our care?"

"There is more to that statement than just her safety, isn't there?" Luke asked.

"Fucking Dom bastard." Garth smiled at his friend. He should have known that his fellow Doms would pick up on how he and Derrick felt about Justine.

"She's attracted to both of you. Did you think I didn't see the way she moved closer to you when you introduced her to us? Both Matt and I gave her the once over, but she only had eyes for you."

Of course he had seen she was attracted to him and Derrick. He wouldn't be much of a Dom if he hadn't. But she had been independent for so long, he wondered if she would trust them enough to really let go and let them into her heart.

"Yeah, but is she willing to give up that control and be with us?"

Chapter Six

Justine wondered why Garth hadn't brought Matt and Luke inside yet. She had a bad feeling in her stomach and although she wanted to go out to see what was happening she stayed where she was, on the sofa snuggled up to Derrick's side. It had been so long since someone had held her and made her feel safe and she wanted to stay in his arms for as long as possible. But her mind was conflicting with her heart, because she knew eventually she would have to go back home and she would be alone once more.

She looked up when the men came into the living room and saw that Matt only had a small bag in his hand and wondered why he hadn't packed up more of her things. If she was going to be staying with Derrick and Garth for any length of time, she was going to need way more clothes than was in that bag.

Her stomach clenched and a lump of anxiety formed inside, making her insides churn and feel tight and heavy. Garth looked at her and she could tell he was angry.

Is he angry at me? What have I done to deserve his anger?

Matt dropped the bag on the floor and she shifted her gaze to Garth when he began walking toward her. He squatted down in front of her and took her hands in his. Derrick helped her to sit up straight, using his body to nudge her, and she clutched at Garth's hands and watched as he closed his eyes for a moment. It looked like Garth was trying to gather his thoughts before opening his mouth. When he finally looked at her again, she felt like she was drowning in his beautiful eyes and blinked to circumvent the effect he had on her.

"Justine, we think Bart may have been at your house." Garth paused and took a deep breath then exhaled slowly. "Baby, he destroyed nearly all of your things. What's in the bag was all that Matt and Luke could find that wasn't damaged."

Justine didn't say anything, she couldn't. Tears began to roll down her face. She had worked so hard for all the material things she had gathered over the years. She knew it was stupid to cry, because stuff could be replaced, even if it would take her a long time, but she just couldn't manage to contain her emotions. She had lost her brother and although he hadn't been much of sibling, he was all she had. But now this.

"Ah, baby, don't cry." Garth released her hands and then scooped her up from the lounge. When he sat down he placed her on his lap and held her tight. She buried her head into his chest and hugged him back. Garth rocked her and just held her until she had her emotions back under control. She heard Derrick and the other two men go into the kitchen, and was glad to have some time alone to get herself back under control.

Garth kissed her head, pushed back a little, and then wiped the moisture from her face. "I know you're grieving right now, but I promise everything will work out in the long run, honey. Derrick and I will buy you some clothes and when this is all over and if you want to move back home, then we'll make sure you have everything you need."

"You can't buy…"

"Shh, baby, you can't stop us, so don't bother arguing." Garth helped her to her feet when the doorbell rang. "That'll be the pizza. Why don't you go into the kitchen and help Derrick get out some drinks?"

Justine watched Garth walk to the door. He looked back over his shoulder and nodded her in the direction of the kitchen, so she hurried to the other room. She figured he didn't want the pizza guy seeing her, since the fewer people who knew where she was hiding out, the better. She helped Derrick get out the plates, napkins and glasses, and got the iced tea from the fridge. Garth came in just as she placed the jug on the table.

The men discussed work while they ate and even though she didn't join in the conversation, she listened avidly and picked up a few more things about their business. By the time everyone had finished eating, Justine was exhausted. She presumed she was just emotionally wrung out and knew a good night's sleep would help, but she didn't want to be alone at the moment. So when they all adjourned to the living room, she sat on the sofa between Derrick and Garth. The movie was just beginning when Garth wrapped an arm around her shoulders and pulled her in until she was resting against his side. She inhaled deeply, breathing in his subtle citrusy cologne, which did nothing to hide the smell of his wonderful, natural masculine aroma. Justine could have spent the rest of her life smelling Derrick and Garth, they smelled that good to her.

A shiver of apprehension shot through her when she realized that she was falling for them. They had taken such good care of her and she'd never had that before. Even though she had only known them for a very short time, she was scared that she was falling in love with them, and she had no idea how to handle that.

* * * *

Derrick was aware the moment Justine fell asleep. It was only about fifteen minutes into the movie, but she had been through so much in the last twenty-four to forty-eight hours and was obviously exhausted. He knew she was the right woman for him and Garth. They had been looking for a sub they could love and spend the rest of their lives with for over five years and he had just about given up hope of ever finding the right woman. When she had walked into their shared office, his cock hard gone rock hard so quickly he was scared he would pass out from lack of oxygen to the brain.

She was smart and fucking sexy, and she wasn't a pushover, and for that he was thankful. Neither he nor Garth wanted a slave twenty-four-seven. They liked a woman who knew her own mind and who would stand up for herself. The thought of telling a woman what to wear and do throughout the day left him cold, but there would be none of that with Justine. She was perfect for them. Now all they had to do was convince her of that.

As they'd watched the movie, he thought over a way to tap into her sexuality and make her let go around them. He wanted to take her to Club of Dominance and introduce her to the world of BDSM. Justine was definitely a submissive and sensual woman, but her passion hadn't been woken as yet and Derrick planned to be one of the men to waken her dormant libido. So far they'd only had a glimpse of her desire, but he knew there was so much more she kept hidden.

Derrick thought about picking Justine up and putting her to bed, but he vetoed that idea as soon as it crossed his mind. He didn't want to disturb her and besides, he liked being up close and personal with her. When he and Garth had realized she was asleep, they had carefully moved her until her head was pillowed on his brother's thigh and he had lifted her legs up and over his. Justine's ass was up against the side of his thigh and he draped an arm over her limbs. "I want to take her to the club," Derrick said quietly so he wouldn't wake Justine.

Matt rose to his feet and stretched. "We are going to head home. We've got an early start tomorrow. Don't get up, you'll wake Justine. We can see ourselves out and I'll make sure the door is locked. See you tomorrow."

Derrick thanked them for their help and then waved his friends off and waited until he heard the door lock click before he relaxed and focused on the movie. But the whole time his eyes were on the TV screen he was more aware of Justine than the movie. Garth drew his attention as he pushed a button on the remote and turned all the equipment off.

"I want to take Justine to the club, too, but we have to give her time to get used to us before we do that. I don't want to frighten her away."

"Yeah, I hear you." Derrick caressed his hand over her thigh. "How long do you want to give her?"

"The swelling and most of the bruising should be gone in a week. Do you think that will be long enough for her to become comfortable around us?"

"Think so, but we'll have to play it by ear. Make sure you watch her body language, and she'll tell us when she's ready, even if she isn't aware of it."

"I want her verbal agreement to be with us before we make another move on her." Garth brushed a strand of hair away from her face. "She has to know her own mind before we take her. I don't want her to have any reason to regret us being with her."

"I don't either." Derrick gently lifted her legs and moved out from beneath her. "It's time to get our woman to bed. She'll be more comfortable lying down between us."

Derrick carefully lifted Justine into his arms and then carried her down the hall toward the master bedroom. Neither he nor Garth had ever used the main bedroom in their house. When they had built it they had wanted to leave that room pristine until they had the woman of their dreams to share it with. Now that they had found Justine and knew she was the one woman meant for them, Derrick had no compunction about taking her there. As soon as he had picked her up, Garth had rushed ahead. The covers were already pulled back and all he needed to do to get her comfortable was remove her clothes, which he did with his brother's help. They left her bra and panties on. Even though he thought her body was a work of art, he knew she wasn't yet completely comfortable being naked around them and he would respect that, especially while she was vulnerable in sleep. What amazed him was the fact that not once did Justine stir. When she slept she crashed and was totally oblivious to everything around her. He covered her with the quilt but kept his eyes on her as he removed his own clothes.

There was no way in hell he was letting her sleep alone, not with that asshole, Bart, still running free. For all he knew, they could have been followed home from the office or Bart could have been lying in wait at her rental and followed Matt and Luke to their house. Although he was sure his friends would have kept watch for a tail and tried to lose them if they had been followed, but there was always a chance that a shadow could be missed. Derrick pushed his turmoil aside and climbed into bed with Justine. He smiled when she immediately scooted over to him until her back was pressing against his side. He turned over and pressed his front to her back and wrapped an arm around her waist. She sighed in her sleep and then her breathing evened out again. Garth got in on the other side and moved closer to her, until his back was up against her front. She was safe and sound in between them right where she should be and Derrick felt his heart fill up with emotion. The feelings were so strong he wanted to spend the night making love with her to show her how much she meant to him but she needed sleep more. He was content for the first time in such a long while, and he had no intention of losing that. He would do everything within his power to work his way into her heart until she couldn't imagine a life without him and his brother at her side.

* * * *

Bart stood in amongst the bushes just outside the property. He'd followed the two men from the house on his motorbike but had made sure to stay far enough back from them that he wouldn't be noticed. And when they had turned into the driveway, he had continued on so they wouldn't be suspicious of him. Half a mile down the road, he pulled over and secured his bike behind a large tree and then jogged back to the house. The two men who had been in Justine's house talked with another man on the porch for a while and then they had all gone inside.

He'd walked down the driveway, staying in the shadows of the small trees lining the drive. He'd been lucky enough that the security gates still stood open, and he scanned for evidence of any other security. Bart cursed in his mind when he saw the elaborate setup. If he hadn't spotted the cameras when he did, he was sure he would have set off an alarm. But maybe not, since the gates to the property were still wide open.

He could see into the kitchen and although he saw people moving around, he couldn't see who it was. One of the people was much shorter, so he figured it had to be Justine, but he wanted to make sure. Bart lifted his binoculars to his eyes, spent a bit of time adjusting the lenses, and then nearly gasped when he saw Justine's face. She was standing at the window, but another man he'd not seen yet was by her side.

He couldn't keep his eyes off of her and had spent the last five years lusting after the sweet and naïve woman. He'd had a lot of one-night stands and every time he fucked he always imagined he was fucking Justine. Over the last six months that hunger had grown to massive proportions and the easy lays he had just weren't cutting it anymore.

Bart cursed under his breath and adjusted his throbbing cock. He'd tried everything he could to get a minute alone with Justine, but Mark must have been suspicious and had always hung around when he was at home. Until the other night. He'd sent Mark out on an urgent delivery for him and the asshole should have been gone for at least three hours, but the bastard must have lain in wait, because he'd barely been gone twenty minutes before he arrived back home. There was no way the prick could have delivered the goods for him, and because he'd ended up killing the fucker, he didn't know where the drugs were. If he didn't find them soon and get the cash for the product, his supplier was going to come after him.

He was going to have to figure out a way to stay alive. Maybe he could tell them that Justine had the goods? Yeah, that sounded like a plan. At least he would stay alive until the assholes found out he was lying. If his supplier believed him, then they would find a way to get hold of her, and then he would be able to step in and save her. He dropped the binoculars and rubbed his hands together as the scenario played out in his mind. Justine would be so grateful to him for saving her that she would probably do anything to show her gratitude.

Bart walked back toward the road, once again staying in the shadows and out of range of the security cameras. He had no idea how he was going to get back on the property if needed, but if his plans succeeded, that wouldn't be necessary.

Chapter Seven

Justine was staring at the bedroom ceiling when Garth entered the room.

"How did you sleep, baby? How do you feel?"

She glanced toward him and then to the hand that held an aromatic cup of coffee. Garth walked closer, placed the mug on the bedside table, and sat down on the side of the bed.

"I'm okay," she replied automatically and then realized the words she had spoken were actually true. She remembered struggling to keep her eyes open as they all watched a movie and nothing after that, so she figured she must have fallen asleep. Garth or Derrick had obviously carried her to bed.

Justine used her arms to maneuver up the bed until her back was resting on the pillow between her and the headboard, but she made sure to keep the covers over her chest. She'd felt that she was only wearing her underwear and wasn't about to go flashing her body around. Although after what she had shared with Derrick and Garth she shouldn't be feeling vulnerable in her state of undress, but she wasn't used to going around in front of others barely clad.

"You're looking a little better. Falling asleep early last night did you a world of good. The dark smudges beneath your eyes aren't so prominent. I'm just glad that you slept the night through. You obviously needed the rest."

"Gee, thanks," Justine muttered and reached for the coffee mug.

"I didn't mean that the way it sounded." Garth gave her a chagrinned smile. "We're both worried about you, Justine.

"And how would you know whether I slept all night?"

"Derrick and I slept in this bed right beside you."

"You did?" She heard the breathless quality of her own voice and hoped he hadn't. The thought of them sleeping beside her, all night long, ramped up her libido. Her breasts swelled and her nipples hardened and that wasn't all. Her pussy clenched and her clit began to throb.

"You have no reason to be worried about me." She paused to sip her coffee. "You're my employers."

Garth reached out for her free hand and threaded his fingers with hers. "We would like to be so much more than that to you, baby. I thought you realized that."

"Is that because of what I initiated yesterday?" Justine felt her cheeks heat and hoped she wasn't as red as she felt. Even though she tried to keep her eyes on his, she couldn't. She looked down at the quilt and waited for his answer.

"No," Garth replied emphatically and reached out to cup her face so that she was once more looking him in the eyes. "Derrick and I were attracted to you from the very beginning. We'd like to be able to explore a relationship with you, but don't for one minute think that your decision will affect your employment or the way we treat you.

"We've already told you that we are Dominants, but what we haven't told you is that you are a submissive. You have all the traits, Justine. You want to please everyone else first and you always put yourself last, but we know you aren't a pushover either. If we pushed you too hard, you would find that inner fire and stand up to us. You are the woman we have been waiting for, and if you allowed yourself to trust us, we could show you more pleasure than you can ever dream of.

"Yesterday afternoon was a small sample of the ecstasy we can give you, but even that would be surpassed if you could open your heart and mind to us. Derrick and I want to take you a BDSM club and show you what you've been missing out on." Garth released her chin and held up his hand, palm out when she opened her mouth to speak. "No, don't answer yet. I want you to take some time to think over what I've said. We'll wait for as long as necessary. Now, why don't you take your coffee into the bathroom and get ready. Derrick hung your clothes up in the closet last night and your underwear is in the top drawer of the dresser. Breakfast should be ready by the time you've finished showering."

Justine watched Garth as he walked out of the room without looking back. *Is he right? Am I a submissive?*

She thought back over her life and realized what Garth said about her trying to please others before herself was true. She'd never caused any trouble while in foster care and had in fact worked really hard, trying to stay in the background by being the perfect child. She did what she was told when she was told.

Although she was very attracted to Derrick and Garth she didn't know if she was brave enough to get into a relationship with them. Would she survive if they broke up? She was scared to lean on them and become too dependent. Trusting them was easy enough. She already did, but to open up to them completely with her heart and soul was another story. If she became dependent on them and they left, she wasn't sure she would be able to go back to the automaton she'd been. It hurt too much to care for someone else but she was so tired of carrying the load and having no one to share the burden. Would she be able to put the pieces of her heart back together if everything fell apart?

And how the hell did he and Derrick know that she was the woman they had been waiting for? They had only met a couple of days ago. As far as she was concerned, it was way too early to know whether they would make a suitable couple. Make that trio. That was another thing she needed to get her head around. How could a relationship between two men, and brothers at that, work when there was only one woman? There was so much to think about and at the moment Justine felt like her rumination was going around in circles. With a sigh, she pushed the covers back and headed toward the bathroom. She was going to have to ask a lot of questions before she even considered getting into a relationship with two men.

And even as she tried to think of what to ask while she showered, the yearning to be with them, to have them love her and help carry the load of everyday living was a hankering she didn't want to ignore. But it wasn't just the thought of having the workload shared. She coveted being in a relationship with the Jackson brothers because they had already begun to work their way into her heart. How could she not have feelings for two sexy hot, muscular men who seemed hell bent on taking care of her? What woman in her right mind would want to refuse being loved by two men? And not just in the physical element of the relationship. Being loved for who she was deep down inside was a craving she'd had for so long. But was she willing to take a chance and open up with them only to have it all go to hell, like everything else in her life had?

After Justine was dressed, she headed toward the kitchen with the now-empty coffee mug in hand. Derrick was at the stove and placing the last piece of bacon from the pan onto the platter. She walked into the kitchen to help, but Garth intercepted her.

"We have everything under control, baby. If you give me your mug, I'll refill it for you. Go and take a seat."

She handed the mug over and sat at the end of table, which was in the dining part of the informal kitchen/dining room. Derrick snagged the platter off the counter, walked over to place it close to her, then sat down on her left side. Garth brought another plate of food as well as her cup.

"Thanks. I've never had anyone make my morning coffee for me."

"If we had our way, we'd bring you coffee in bed every day." Derrick pushed the heaped platter toward her. "Eat up, honey."

Justine placed some food on the plate in front of her and they ate in a comfortable silence. When they were finished, she rose to her feet and began to clean up. Both men got up to help.

"Thanks for breakfast. I can't remember the last time I ate something I didn't cook."

"You're welcome, Justine, but you didn't eat very much. You're not trying to watch your weight, are you?" Garth asked.

"No." She rinsed a plate and handed it to Garth to put in the dishwasher. "I've never worried about my weight. It's just that I've been so busy I often forget to eat or just don't have the time to have a meal. I'm used to getting by on little sustenance."

Garth grabbed the next plate but instead of pulling it from her hand he held still. "That is going to change, baby. You need to eat three meals a day and you will take the time out to eat. You have an hour for lunch and I want you to take every minute of that hour to eat and relax. If you don't start taking care of yourself, you're liable to get sick."

Justine was a little taken aback at the steel in Garth's voice but then realized his dominance was coming to the forefront. Instead of feeling angry over his tone and directive, she found her body liked being told what to do. Her nipples hardened and brushed against the lacy material of her bra and her clit ached and pussy spasmed, sending cream dripping out onto her panties. She tried really hard to look away from Garth's gaze, but she couldn't seem to manage the action and felt like she was drowning in his hazel eyes. A slow smile spread across his face and then he gave her a salacious wink and finally removed the plate from her hand. Justine drew in a deep breath and turned back to the sink.

She was aching with desire and wanted to say to hell with the consequences and jump in with both feet, but knew she needed more time before she did anything rash. Maybe she should let them take her to their club. The idea had merit. Surely seeing them in a different environment, other than their place of business or home would give her more of an insight into their personalities. It was a scary thing to even speculate about. What if they wanted to whip her?

Justine had never thought herself to be into pain and the thought of the two Jackson brothers applying the tail of a whip to her skin didn't turn her on in the least, but then she imagined them spanking her ass, and that caused her pussy to clench and release more juices onto her panties.

Oh God. What is wrong with me? You've got to stop thinking about it and get ready for work.

"All done." Derrick's voice drew her from her thoughts and she realized that she was standing motionless at the sink with the water still running. She turned the tap off and glanced toward Garth from underneath her eyelashes and was thankful he didn't seem to notice she was daydreaming.

"Are you ready to go?"

She turned to face Derrick. "I just need to brush my teeth again and grab my purse."

"Then hop to it, woman," Derrick ordered, smiling.

As she hurried past he slapped her on the ass, eliciting a gasp from her, and although she wanted to turn and ask why he had done it, she wasn't feeling that brave at the moment. Especially since she wanted to ask him to do it again and again. That small smack had caused tingles to reverberate from her ass to her cunt and she was in danger of begging them to make love to her, but she was nowhere near ready to take that step. At least not yet.

* * * *

Justine had been working steadily throughout the day, answering e-mails and sending out quotes. She enjoyed her job and hoped she could spend the next few years working for the Jackson brothers.

She looked up when Matt and Luke came strolling down the hall from where they had been working in the monitoring room and she greeted each man. They replied then hurried into the office and closed the door behind them. Both men had been polite, but Justine had seen the anger on their faces and wondered what was going on. She gave a shrug of her shoulders and concentrated on costing the next quote. When she looked up again, she realized it was past the time she should have started her lunch break, so she saved the files she was working on and hibernated her computer screen.

Matt and Luke came out of the office with Derrick and Garth behind them. The Plant brothers nodded in her direction and then headed back to the control room. Garth and Derrick stopped beside her and looked at her expectantly.

Derrick's eyes jumped down to the purse in Justine's hand. "You going to lunch?"

"Yes, just about to head out."

Derrick smiled approvingly. "Perfect. We're heading out for something to eat, too. Why don't we all go together? It's safer that way."

"Okay."

"Good." Derrick took her hand and began to lead her toward the door. Garth rushed around them and held the door open for her. That courteous little action caused her to fall a little more for the two men who seemed to want to help her in any way they could. Tears pricked the back of her eyes and she had to blink a few times to dispel the moisture. She should have known that the Jackson brothers would see her emotion. They noticed nearly every little thing she did and the more they looked out for and took care of her, the faster she was falling under their spell.

Derrick tugged on her hand and pulled her closer to the buildings, out of the pedestrians' way. Garth moved in behind her until his front rested against her back and she could feel the heat emanating from his body. Still gripping her hand, Derrick used his free hand and nudged her chin with a knuckle until she met his brown-eyed gaze. "What's wrong, honey?"

"Nothing," Justine replied and frowned, hoping he would take the facial expression as confusion. She should have known better.

"Don't lie to me, Justine. When your Dom asks you a question, we expect to be answered honestly."

"You're not my Dom," Justine said in a low voice so that the people walking past wouldn't hear her.

"You're right. We aren't your Doms," Garth said against her ear. His warm, moist breath caressed her sensitive flesh causing her to shiver. "But we hope to change that situation very soon."

"We'll have that discussion after work." Derrick glared at Garth but his expression eased when he looked back at her. "Now answer my question but this time, be truthful."

Justine went to lower her head but wasn't able to as Derrick still had a finger beneath her chin, so she glanced off to the side. She took a fortifying breath and met his gaze again. "You and Garth do such nice things for me and since I'm not used to that it made me a little emotional."

Garth wrapped an arm around her waist and kissed the side of her neck. "Thank you for answering the question. We like taking care of you, baby. Try to imagine what it would be like if you stayed with us."

Derrick finally released her chin and then he cupped her cheek as he stared at her intently. "We like making you feel good, honey. We want to do that for the rest of our lives."

Justine's stomach let out a loud growl, reminding them all of the reason they were standing on the sidewalk. Derrick laughed and lowered the hand near her face as Garth stepped away from behind her. Without their bodies so close to her, she felt almost bereft and cold. She was getting used to them being close by. They had cuddled with her on the sofa the previous evening and slept in the same bed. It was getting harder and harder for her to imagine going through life without the two Jackson brothers at her side.

Chapter Eight

Garth watched Justine over lunch and had to bite back a smile of satisfaction. She was beginning to care for him and Derrick and he couldn't wait to introduce her into the world of BDSM. Her reactions to them the previous evening let him know that he was right in his way of thinking. Their woman had already shown them that she trusted them with her body to a certain extent after begging them to make love with her yesterday afternoon, and each action henceforth had proven to him time and again that she was comfortable with him and Derrick.

The way she had snuggled up with him and Derrick on the sofa after dinner last night, and the way she had draped over first him and his brother intermittently throughout the night while sharing the bed with her was another affirmation of her trust. Her body language was very easy to read but her mind hadn't caught up with her instincts or her heart as yet. It was only a matter of time before she relented and let them make love with her.

Garth knew damn well he could seduce her into accepting them both but he wasn't about to do that. He wanted her coming to them willingly without any coercion on their behalf, because then she would have no reason to blame them if she pulled back from them. They were going to have to make Justine aware that once she accepted them there would be no second thoughts.

Justine was currently frowning down at her glass as she swallowed the last of her iced tea. The waitress had taken their drink orders but Garth had asked for time to think over what they wanted for lunch. He wanted to spend as much uninterrupted time talking with Justine as he could and he knew Derrick felt the same way.

"What are you thinking about, baby?"

She swallowed then wiped her mouth with a napkin. "How can a relationship with one woman and two men work?"

Derrick turned in his seat to face Justine. "The men have to be very good friends and trust each other for a start. There can't be any jealousy involved where they are concerned."

"Secondly," Garth said, "communication is the key. There should be no secrets between any of the people involved in the relationship. Derrick and I are best friends as well as brothers and tell each other everything."

"Thirdly," Derrick said quietly so no one could hear their conversation, "the woman can never try to pit us against each other. If we catch our woman playing one of us against the other, we'll punish her."

Justine lowered her eyes and shifted in her seat. Garth looked over at Derrick and saw the desire and amusement in his brother's eyes and knew his expression was probably the same. Justine was turned on by the idea of punishment and trying to hide it, but at least she was finally asking questions. If her curiosity was piqued, then she had to be interested enough about the schematics of a ménage relationship to warrant asking about it. Didn't she? *God, I hope so.*

She pushed her empty glass away and looked at him and then Derrick before coming back to him again. "But what if one of you did get jealous? Wouldn't that cause a rift between the two of you? There is no way I—*she* would want to cause problems between the two of you."

Garth reached out and placed his hand over hers, which was resting on the tabletop, and squeezed gently. "That would never happen, baby. Derrick and I have always known we would share a woman once we met the right one. We've had a couple of ménage relationships, but for one reason or another it never worked out."

"Why not?" Justine asked.

"The first woman we tried to have a relationship with was only in it for the thrill of having a threesome." Derrick paused to take a sip of coffee. "It turns out she was in it for the sex. Apparently she'd always wanted to have sex with two guys and we were only a fling for her."

"That must have hurt." Justine frowned.

"At the time," Garth answered honestly, "but it was our damaged ego and not our hearts that took a beating. We were too young back then to realize we were being played, but we're more experienced now and know what we are feeling and what we want."

Garth wondered if she realized what he had just told her, but wasn't about to lay his heart totally on the line until Justine had made up her mind about what she wanted. If he told her how he really felt, she would either run for the hills or wouldn't believe him.

"The second woman liked to pit us against each other. It took a while for Derrick and me to realize what was happening, but when we did we sat down and talked to her. She decided it was too much hard work to be with two men and broke it off."

"Were you in love with her?"

"No," Derrick and Garth answered at the same time.

Garth could see her mind was working overtime but he stayed silent so she could process what they had told her. When she was ready, she would ask more questions.

"What type of punishment?"

Garth's cock went from semi-hard to full mast in zero point two seconds. It was a wonder he didn't get dizzy from lack of blood to his brain. He could see Justine secured to a spanking bench or to a St. Andrew's Cross while he and Derrick punished her until she begged them to come. He pushed his lust aside when Derrick began to respond.

"If our woman needed to be punished, we would tie her down and spank her bare ass until it turned a nice, pretty pink color." Derrick cleared his throat but he kept his gaze on Justine. "And we wouldn't stop until she was begging us to come."

Garth watched in fascination as the color in her cheeks heightened and then she shifted in her seat once more. He looked down at her chest and nearly groaned out loud when he spied her prominent nipples poking against the red blouse she was wearing. He wanted to place his fingers and thumbs over those turgid peaks and squeeze until she gasped out with pleasure and then he wanted to slip his hands down the front of her trousers and under her panties and feel the wetness between her pussy lips. She was already turned on. He could smell the cream leaking from her cunt.

Garth drained the last of his coffee to ease the dryness in his throat and took over from Derrick. "If our woman had been really bad, we could bring her to the edge of climax over and over again and not let her come until she was screaming."

"Oh God," Justine whimpered.

Garth glanced around the diner quickly and realized that most of the lunch crowd was gone. There was an elderly man sitting at the counter, talking to the waitress, and other than the cook out back, the place looked empty. They had been lucky enough to get a booth in the back of the restaurant that was situated so that the tall seat backs obscured the three of them from the view of the other customers. That would come in handy.

The waitress approached and took their orders, refilled their drinks and once she was gone, Garth moved in close to her side and draped his arm over her shoulders.

Justine turned her head to look at him and asked in a whisper, "What are you doing?"

Derrick moved in on the other side of her, until they were both plastered against the sides of her body.

Garth held her gaze and slowly lowered his head. He kissed her lightly on the lips and sighed into her mouth when she opened up to him without any hesitation. While he kept her mouth occupied by slipping his tongue inside and tangling it with hers, he pulled on her shirt until it came out of the waistband of her pants. He caressed his fingers over the smooth, soft skin of her belly. Justine turned her head away from his and gulped in air. She had taken two deep breaths and then Derrick was kissing her.

He flicked the button on her pants open, slid the zipper down, and then slid his hand into her panties. Biting his lip was the only way to hold in his lustful groan when he encountered her hot, wet cunt. Turning slightly so he had the diner's occupants in his peripheral vision, he pressed two fingers into her vagina and placed his thumb over her clit. When he saw movement beneath her shirt, he knew that Derrick was playing with her nipples and was very glad his brother was still kissing her when she mewled with pleasure.

Garth began to pump his fingers in and out of her pussy and although she tried to stay quiet, he could hear the small muffled sounds of pleasure she made. When he curled his fingers inside her and found her G-spot, he kept rubbing over the spongy flesh while he thrummed her clit. Her fingers reached down and gripped his wrist firmly and he knew she was on the edge of an orgasm. Since he wanted her to explode like she never had before he stopped his movements and waited until her internal walls stopped rippling around his digits. Her grip on him relaxed, and he held in a chuckle as he started all over again. He thrust his fingers in and out of her cunt, pushing in as far as the webbing of his hand and then withdrew only to do it again and again. Her muscles clenched on him again, and this time he wasn't sure if it was to egg him on or because she was climbing the ladder to ecstasy again. Not that it mattered. He wasn't about to let her control what her body did.

Once more he stilled and waited for the tension in her muscles to wane. She slumped and then Garth hooked his fingers once more and massaged the pads of his fingers over her sweet spot while caressing her clit with his thumb. He leaned in close to her ear and nipped her earlobe. "Come now, Justine."

Her pussy tightened around his fingers, squeezing so hard he couldn't contain the groan that formed in his chest from rumbling up and escaping through his mouth. Thank God Derrick had leaned down to cover her mouth with his again, because if he hadn't, the other occupants of the diner would have known what they were up to. The moan Justine made as she came was muffled enough not to be heard by anyone but himself and Derrick. Little aftershocks rippled through her pussy intermittently until finally Justine's body relaxed and slumped against his side. With gentle care for her sensitive sex, he slowly withdrew his fingers from her cunt and then removed them from her pants. Derrick released her mouth and she was panting as she turned toward him.

Justine was looking at him with satiated glazed eyes and he couldn't resist teasing her a little more. He lifted his arm and then shoved the fingers that had just been in her vagina into his mouth and sucked them clean. Her gasp was audible and her breath hitched as her eyes turned hungry again. Garth had known that their woman was hiding her passionate side and her reaction to him confirmed his suspicions. And they had barely tapped into her desire. He couldn't wait to get her to the club and show her how really responsive she truly was, but he wasn't sure she would agree to going there. She was an introvert in some ways, but Garth knew once they had really unleashed the fiery woman inside, there would be no going back. Now all he and Derrick had to do was convince her to trust them with her heart as she did with her body.

* * * *

Justine came out of her renewed lust-induced haze when the waitress at the counter dropped something on the floor. Whatever it was broke with a resounding smash. With shaking fingers she zipped up her pants and fastened the button. She wanted to tuck her blouse back into her pants, but since she was sitting down that task would prove a little difficult. She pushed against Derrick's arm, trying to get him to move, but didn't look up into his face.

Why she had let them get her off in a public place was beyond her. She had never done anything so risky in her life. She felt a little embarrassed that the two men could seduce her enough with words that she let all her inhibitions go, not caring where she was.

"What's wrong, honey?" Derrick asked.

"I–I need to use the bathroom."

Derrick moved out of the booth and stepped back so she could get out. Again she kept her eyes down and hurried toward the restroom. She caught her reflection in the mirror and groaned. Her cheeks were flushed and her lips looked swollen from all the kissing. Her shirt was creased around the bottom and it hung down around her hips. Turning away from the mirror, she hurried into a stall to clean up. Once she was all tucked in again, she washed her hands, splashed some cold water on her face, then patted it dry with some paper towel. Her eyes still looked a little dreamy and her lips were still puffy, but at least she no longer looked like she had just been brought to orgasm where anyone could have seen.

She glared at herself in the mirror. "What the hell do you think you were doing, girl? Shit, do you have no shame?" But then her thought process changed from rebuking to embracing. There was nothing wrong with what she had just let happen. The feelings she had for the two Jackson brothers were already running deep. The attraction she had for them was so strong she couldn't resist them anymore, and when they had begun describing how they would punish her—she wasn't stupid and knew they had been talking about her—her libido had raged to a flaming inferno. She was just glad that Derrick and Garth had made sure the waitress and patrons hadn't heard her moans of pleasure as they had gotten her off.

Justine straightened her shoulders and lifted her head high. She was more than curious about going to their club and finding out what the fuss was about. She'd heard about BDSM but hadn't thought much about it, but when they had told her what they wanted to do to her she'd been so turned on she was ready to jump their bones. She'd trusted them with her body, but could she trust them with her heart?

Stop being such a coward, Justine. You won't ever know what could be if you don't open up with them. Do you want to spend the rest of your life alone and lonely?

Nah, ah, not happening. Been there done that since you were eleven years old. It's about time you grabbed hold of what's on offer and don't let go. With her resolve firmly in place she headed back out into the diner.

Derrick and Garth looked up as she approached. They looked tense but they didn't speak. They looked at her almost expectantly. Justine decided to wait until the end of the work day to tell her men what she had decided. It was going to be hard enough to get through the rest of the day as it was, let alone if they knew she was willing to explore her submissive side with them.

As she took her seat at the booth, she realized the food had arrived while she was in the bathroom. They had waited for her to get back before they started on theirs, and she smiled at their tense expressions before she started on her meal. They ate in silence, but she didn't mind. She got a secret pleasure out of her newfound power and her ability to keep them in suspense. She'd tell them her decision when the time was right, and it wouldn't kill them to wait until that moment. Once they were finished the men were looking edgier than ever.

She moved her napkin from her lap onto the table. "Are you ready to head back to the office?"

The muscles in Garth's jaw ticked, but he slid out of the booth. Derrick got out on the other side and she noticed that his hands were clenched into fists. They were such dominant, confident men, but seeing them unsure of themselves only endeared them more to her.

Justine felt feminine and powerful for the first time. She'd never been aware of her own sexuality or feminine wiles before. It was a heady experience.

Garth left money on the table to cover their bill, as well as a good tip, and then led the way out. Derrick was at her back and his eyes were traveling over her body. Tingles and prickles of awareness erupted everywhere his gaze touched and she couldn't help but tease him by putting a little extra sway in her hips. None of them spoke as they walked back to the office and Justine knew she couldn't leave them in any doubt after what had happened back in the diner.

Garth held the door to the building open and then he and Derrick moved around her and into their office. Derrick was about to close the door, but she placed her hand on the wood and saw the surprise on his face. He had obviously expected her to get straight back to work.

"Can I talk to you and Garth for a moment, please?"

Derrick stepped back and pulled the door wider and swept his arm out in silent invitation. Justine headed for a chair that was positioned between and in front of their two desks. The door to the office closed with a resounding click and she took a deep breath to calm her nerves.

The Jackson brothers were right. She was a submissive and she had spent most of her life hiding away her true self in the hope of pleasing others. Well, that had to change and right now. She was sick and tired of putting her needs on the back burner just to keep others happy.

She wanted to know what it was like to feel and to be placed first for a change. Derrick and Garth had showed her a small taste of what it would be like with them. They had put her needs first and hadn't once taken advantage of her even when she was hurt and grieving for her brother. She craved more. So much more.

She wanted it all and she was going to take it.

Chapter Nine

Derrick moved around to lean against the front of Garth's desk and waited to hear what Justine had to say. He was scared they had pushed her too hard and fast when they had made her come in the diner. When she'd scurried away to the bathroom afterward his chest had tightened into a knot of anxiety and it still hadn't let go.

What worried him the most was the resolve he'd seen in her eyes. *Is she going to resign and tell us to go to hell?*

Garth came out from behind his desk and sat beside him. His brother crossed his arms over his chest and he fisted his hands.

"No," Justine said quietly, stopping Derrick before he could start speaking. "Let me talk and when I've finished you can have your turn."

Derrick nodded.

"I've only recently realized that I have been running from life and lying to myself. You see, I am a submissive and have dealt with that the only way I knew how. I've always put others' needs before mine and let people use my personality against me, let them run roughshod over me. Part of that is the submissive in me, but I know I'm better than that. I let my brother and Bart use me and although I occasionally tried to stand up for myself, I didn't try very hard. I'm better than that. You two have shown me that.

"You and Garth have shown me I don't have to be that way. You've put my needs first and taken care of me. I have feelings for you both and at first that scared the hell out of me. But today in the diner opened my eyes." She looked each of them in the eye and then rose to her feet.

Derrick had no idea where she was heading with her little speech, but the knot of tension in his gut had abated and his heart began to feel hopeful.

"When you began to answer my questions about BDSM, you knew I was aroused. Instead of ignoring my needs you satisfied my body but you made sure that no one was aware of what was happening." She looked toward Garth. "I saw the way you used your body to shield me from prying eyes, and for that I'm grateful. And I'm also grateful to you"—she looked at Derrick—"for making sure no one heard me. What you did to me in a public place where we could have been caught excited me beyond reason.

"Not once have either of you tried to take advantage of me, and if you still want to, I want to explore this thing between us. I want to go to your club with you. I want more."

Derrick walked over to Justine and pulled her into his arms. She sighed and leaned her body against him, trusting him to keep her upright. His heart filled with love and he knew without a doubt that Justine was their woman. He couldn't wait to introduce her to BDSM and show her how much pleasure they could give and, in return, how much pleasure it would give him and Garth.

"Thank you, honey. We promise to show you delights beyond your imagination. Your heart is safe with us, Justine."

Garth moved around behind her, wrapped his arms around her waist and kissed the top of her head. "You won't regret your decision, baby. We will never do anything to hurt you."

"I know," Justine replied and pulled back from Derrick. Garth moved away and she gave them each a smile before she started walking toward the door. "I'd better get back to work. I'll see you when we're finished."

Derrick waited until she closed the door behind her before turning to Garth. "Thank God. I thought she was going to fucking quit and walk out."

"Me, too." Garth pushed his fingers through his hair and sighed. "I've never been so scared in my life."

"Me either." Derrick moved back around his desk and sat down. "Now, what the hell are we going to do about this fucker Bart? Two of the boys on night shift swear they saw him lurking around outside the back of the office at the far edge of the parking lot, but since he was so far away from the security camera, and the asshole was wearing a cap, they aren't certain."

"I have a bad feeling about that asshole. He's going to try something soon."

"Yeah, I have the same feeling. We can't call the cops every time we think we see him. They will get mighty sick and tired of hearing from us if he takes off before they can get here."

"I know." Garth scrubbed a hand over his face. "We'll just have to make sure Justine is never left alone. That way the asshole can't get near her, and if he's stupid enough to try, he has to go through us first."

"We're gonna have to start wearing our guns all the time," Derrick said.

"I already am." Garth pulled the side of his jacket open to show Derrick the pistol in the holster strapped to his shoulder.

Derrick grinned and did the same. There was no way in hell they were going to be unprepared. Justine was the love of his life and he suspected Garth's, too. They would keep her safe no matter what.

"There's not much we can do about that prick until he shows his hand." Garth reached for the phone on his desk. "I'm going to order a few things for our sub. I want her to be able to dress appropriately."

"Order some toys while you're at it."

"Good idea. Shit, tonight isn't going to come fast enough. I wanted to haul her out of here and to our apartment upstairs to make love with her."

"I did, too. We've waited for her our whole adult lives. I'm sure we can survive another few hours," Derrick said.

"It'll be touch and go, man."

"I hear you." Derrick grinned and then grimaced as he adjusted his hard, aching cock in his pants.

* * * *

Justine was excited and nervous at the same time as she stood in the closet, looking for something to wear. The flutters in her belly had been there since she had spoken to Garth and Derrick in their office after lunch. The afternoon had dragged and yet it had gone faster than she thought it would. She was a mass of contradictions and emotions but she was eager to get to their club and find out what all the fuss was about. Would they tie her down and make love to her while others watched? That thought ramped her arousal up another notch. She'd only just had a shower and if she wasn't careful and let her imagination get the best of her she would need another one. Her pussy was already wet and if her thoughts stayed on the same track, she would need to change her underwear.

The door to the bedroom opened. Garth and Derrick entered and both of them had shopping bags in their hands. When they'd had time to go shopping was beyond her. Neither of them had left the office that afternoon, and they had all come straight home. Then she remembered hearing the doorbell while she was taking a shower after dinner. They must have had the stuff delivered.

They walked over to the bed and tossed the bags down. Garth turned to her. "We bought you a few things that are appropriate to wear as our submissive, but before you get dressed we want to shave your pussy."

"What?"

Derrick moved close behind her and wrapped his arms around her waist. She shivered when he splayed one of his large hands over her belly and began caressing her. "We like our women bare, Justine. We want to be able to see your body's response to what we do to you."

"Plus you'll be much more sensitive when we touch you," Garth chimed in.

"But I've already had a shower," Justine said.

"Don't you worry about it, baby. We'll make sure we clean you thoroughly."

"Do you trust us, Justine?" asked Derrick.

"Yes," she answered emphatically and without hesitation, which brought a smile and a possessive gleam into Garth's eyes.

"Good." Garth moved toward the bathroom and Derrick removed his arms from around her waist. Garth was back in moments and tossed a large towel to his brother, but his hands were full of other items that would be needed to shave her.

"Get on the bed, honey." She turned toward Derrick and saw that he had spread the large towel to protect the covers and she climbed up onto it. "Good girl." He leaned over her and placed a light kiss on her lips.

Contentment filled her at his praise and how she felt so good about pleasing him. She wondered if that was part and parcel of a Dom/sub relationship. If so, then she was definitely the right person for these two men. With every passing minute she spent with them, she fell a little more in love with them and she wanted to please them as much as she could. Justine wasn't naïve enough to think they wouldn't have any arguments or tough times in their life if their relationship turned out to be long term, but she was more happy within herself and would have no compunction standing up for herself or to them if she didn't believe they were right, or what they wanted from her wasn't comfortable.

Garth had gone back into the bathroom and once again he returned, but this time he had a steaming bowl of water in his hands. She watched him place it on the bedside table and noticed that there was also a pair of scissors, a razor, and shaving cream on the top.

Derrick climbed onto the bed and tapped her lightly on the thigh. "Spread those legs for me as wide as you can, Jusi."

She liked the nickname Derrick had just called her. Mark and
Brad had called her Jus, but she liked Derrick's name for her better.
With a smile, she lifted her legs up until her knees were bent and her
feet were flat on the mattress. Garth handed him the scissors and a
small plastic bag. She relaxed back on the bed while he began cutting
away her pubic hair. Justine wasn't uncomfortable at being exposed to
him while he worked. In fact she found that she was becoming very
turned on. Each brush of his fingers against her sensitive flesh pushed
her arousal higher. By the time he had finished, her pussy was soaked
with cream as was her asshole.

"I think our woman is enjoying our attention." Derrick's voice
drew her gaze to his and he smiled and then winked at her. He
climbed off the bed, taking the scissors and small trash bag with him.

Garth took his place after grabbing a washcloth out of the bowl
and squeezing most of the water from it. He placed the hot cloth over
her pussy and held it down. Justine gasped at the heat, not because it
was too hot, but because of the blissful sensations when he pushed it
against her mound. She moaned when he added a small amount of
pressure to her mound and clit.

"You like having us touch you, don't you, baby?"

"Yes."

"Good girl. Always answer our questions honestly. The key to
making a ménage relationship work is good communication. I want
you to tell us if you don't like something or if we piss you off. Can
you promise to do that, Justine?"

"Yes."

Derrick came back from the bathroom and sat beside her again.
"You are such a good little sub. Let me explain a few things about
BDSM to you while Garth shaves that pretty little cunt.

"The first and foremost thing to remember is your safe word. All
subs have a word to use that will halt any play or scene if they
become frightened or if play becomes too much to handle. We are
taking you to Club of Dominance. We are friends with the owners and

have a lot of other friends there we like to socialize with. The club safe word is red. You are to use that if you want play to totally stop. Do you understand?"

"Yes," she answered, feeling a little nervous and hoping she wouldn't need to use the safe word but also glad she had a way to stop proceedings if she needed to.

"Good." Derrick stood up and moved closer then sat on the side of the bed and stroked a finger down her cheek. "You can also use the word yellow if you're uncertain about what we are doing to you or what we are about to do to you."

"What is your safe word, sub?" Garth asked as he swiped the razor over her foam-covered folds and mound.

"Red."

"Good," Garth replied. "Now the proper way to address a Dom is Sir or Master. What is the word to use if you are unsure about what we're doing to you?"

"Yellow, Master."

"Very pretty, baby. You're a fast learner. You please me very much."

"Our little sub is going to be a delight to train," Derrick said.

"Yes, she is," Garth responded. "Do you have a problem with nudity, Justine?"

She thought about that before answering. She imagined being nude in front of a lot of other people while Derrick and Garth played with her, and her pussy clenched, releasing another lot of juices.

"What just went through your head, honey?"

"Whatever it was turned her on," Garth said. "She just creamed herself."

Justine thought she should have been embarrassed about the way they were talking about her and her body's responses but their discussion regarding her physical reactions turned her on even more.

"I don't have a problem with nudity, Masters."

"And?" Derrick and Garth looked at her expectantly and she knew she wasn't going to get away without answering the rest of the question.

"I imagined you both playing with me while others watched and it turned me on."

"I'm very pleased with you, sub. You are very brave."

"I'm glad that you're into public exhibition. We want to display you with pride, but don't ever think we would let anyone else touch you."

"That's good, because the thought of someone else touching me is repugnant. Oh, sorry, Masters."

"Nice save, baby. Okay, I'm done, but stay still so I can wipe you off. Then I will show you what you're wearing tonight. Once you're dressed we can leave. Okay?" Garth asked.

"Yes, Master."

It took every ounce of control Justine had not to move and squirm while Garth wiped the rest of the shaving cream and the few stray hairs away from her pussy. By the time he had finished and then patted her dry, she was nearly ready to beg him to make her come.

Garth gathered up the equipment and took it into the bathroom. Derrick helped her up off the bed and then emptied the shopping bags onto the quilt. Justine picked up a dark purple corset and held it up.

"Good choice, Jusi. That color enhances your beautiful long black hair and stormy gray eyes. I think the black skirt and heels will go well together."

"That's the outfit I wanted her to wear tonight," Garth said as he came up behind her. "Put the skirt on, baby."

Justine put the skirt on and pulled the zipper up and then she put the corset on and fastened the hooks in the front. She felt delectably wicked when she caught her men staring at her through hungry eyes. Her breasts were made to look more voluptuous as they were pushed up in the corset and her legs felt longer since the skirt ended mid-thigh. The outfit was so far removed from what she usually wore, but she felt totally feminine and sexy in it.

She moved toward the dresser but was brought to a halt when Garth snagged her around the waist with his arm. "Where are you going?"

"What about panties?"

"When we are going to play, we make all the decisions. Do you agree to that, Justine?"

"Yes, Master."

"Good." Garth kissed her bare shoulder. "You don't get to wear panties unless we tell you to. The Dom part of a D/s relationship is all about control. We like to take command in every aspect of the sexual side of our relationship. That means when we are playing with you, we have total control over what goes on. We will control when you climax and how often. We may even hold back your pleasure as a punishment if you displease us. In other words we get off on controlling you. When a Dom is good at topping a sub, he gets an adrenaline rush and it enhances his pleasure, but don't think we won't be enhancing your own pleasures, too."

"We will always give you what you need, Jusi. Not necessarily what you want," Derrick said. "Do you understand, honey?"

"I think so."

"Put your shoes on and let's go," Garth said. He held her elbow as she stepped into the high-heeled shoes.

They led her toward the front door and she was grateful that they each held onto her hands. She'd worn heels before but never ones this high. She was scared she was going to turn her ankle or fall and end up breaking her neck.

"Don't worry, baby. We won't let you fall."

That was another thing she was going to have to get used to. The two Jackson brothers read her so well it was as if they could read her mind. Of course she knew that was totally ludicrous because there was no such thing as telepathy.

Justine prayed that she wouldn't do anything to embarrass herself or her men. She wanted them to be pleased with her and she wanted to make them proud. There was only one way to see if she was really the woman they needed in their life and if she would be enough for them.

She couldn't help but hope the step that brought her out of the house and onto the front porch was also a step in the right direction for the rest of her life.

Chapter Ten

Justine looked at the ornate door knocker on the large wooden double doors that led to the inside of the club. She gulped audibly when she spied the wrought-iron handles that looked like a coiled whip.

Derrick tugged her to the side of the landing and gripped her shoulders gently. Garth came up behind her until his chest connected with her back. "What just scared you, honey?"

"Uh, the whip." The intonation in her voice was a little higher than normal and made her answer sound more like a question.

"The thought of us whipping you scares the shit out of you, doesn't it, baby?"

"Yes, M–Master."

"We aren't into sadomasochism, Justine. We don't like inflicting hard pain any more than you want to feel it. In fact, the owners of this club have banned anyone into sadomasochism from joining. There are also a lot of Doms who work here as monitors. If you use your safe word, it will bring those monitors running. You're safe with us and in this club, baby. We will spank you with our hands and maybe a paddle, we might use a soft flogger on you, but we will never use a whip on you."

"Remember to use the word yellow if you want a break from play and red if you want to stop altogether, okay?" Derrick asked, but she knew it was a reminder for her so she felt safe.

"Yes, thank you, Masters."

"Are you ready, Jusi?"

"Yes, Master Derrick."

"Very pretty, little sub," he replied and led her inside the foyer of the club.

"Hi, Garth, Derrick," a hulking blond brute behind the reception desk greeted her men. He was so tall and muscular and had an aura of confidence surrounding him just like the Jackson brothers that Justine knew he had to be a Dom. A petite chestnut-haired woman leaning against his side was dressed similarly to her, so she had to be his sub. "Who have you got there?"

"Hi, Tank. This is our sub, Justine Downey. She's new to the scene."

"Hi, Justine, and welcome."

"Thank you."

She knew when the big blond's smile fell she had made a mistake and quickly corrected it. "Thank you, Master Tank."

"Very pretty, little sub." He smiled warmly at her and gave her a wink. "Before long the correct response will be second nature to you. Isn't that right, Emma?"

"Yes, Master." Emma turned to her with a saucy smile and rolled her eyes. Since Master Tank was still watching the woman, he caught her. He moved and then a loud slap sounded and Emma gasped.

"You're just pushing me tonight, baby. Are you wanting my attention?"

"I always want your attention, Master."

"Glad to hear it." Master Tank gave her another swat on the ass. "When Jack and Gary get here, you'll have all the attention you want."

"I can't wait," Emma replied with sass before turning to Justine. She handed over some forms. "You need to read the rules and regulations of the club, Justine. When you're done you need to sign on the dotted line."

Justine took her time reading over the policies and relaxed a little more with each paragraph. Especially when she read about the safe words her men had told her about and the rule about no hard pain.

When she was finished, she reached for the pen and signed and then handed the forms back.

"Have a nice night," Emma said as Derrick and Garth guided her to another set of double doors. At first she was astounded and a little uncomfortable at the sights that greeted her. The room was massive with a large bar across the way. There was a small dance floor, which looked filled to capacity, but it was the raised dais that drew her attention.

A very tiny, slim, blonde-haired woman was secured to what looked like a saw bench, and she was being hit with a small whip with lots of tails on it. Each time the whip connected with her back and ass, she would moan in pleasure. Two men, identical in appearance, stood near the woman. They had light hair and the only difference in their appearance was one of the men wore his hair longer. The man with the shoulder-length hair flung the whip aside, walked up behind the woman, and then drove his cock deep into her pussy. She opened her mouth to scream in pleasure, but the sound was muffled when the other guy shoved his cock in her mouth.

Justine pressed her legs together when her clit began to throb and her pussy clenched, forcing cream out onto the inside of her upper thighs.

"Do you like what you see, baby?" Garth wrapped his arms around her waist and pulled her tight against him. He pushed his hips into her ass and back and left her in no doubt of how turned on he was.

"Yes…yes, Master."

"Would you like to be up there where everyone could see your sexy little body while we fucked you?"

"Yes, Master," she answered breathily.

"Good girl. I'm proud of you, baby."

Justine's heart filled up with joy at pleasing her men. Love swarmed her and she knew she wanted to be with Derrick and Garth for the rest of her life. She turned around to voice her feelings but stopped when two men approached from only yards away. The men came to a stop in front of her and her men.

"Garth, Derrick, we haven't seen you for a while. How have you been?"

"Well, just busy as hell," Garth replied and shook the man's hand. When he released him, Garth turned to her. "Justine, these two men are owners of the club. This is Master Turner Pike and Master Barry Winston."

"I'm pleased to meet you, Masters."

"Welcome, Justine."

"Hi, Justine."

"So what do you think of the club?" Master Turner asked.

"It's interesting. This is my first time in a BDSM club."

"Our sub, Charlie, has only been in the scene for a short time, too, but if you have any questions and want a submissive's point of view, don't hesitate to ask her."

"Thank you, Master."

"Have fun." The Masters wandered off.

"Let's show you around." Master Garth slid his hand down her arm, clasped her hand, and led her along the great room.

Along one side of the large room were a lot of doorways without any doors and the wall was made of glass. Her men guided her to a window and stopped to view the scene.

Inside was a woman on what looked like an OBGYN's table but the woman was strapped down by her wrists and ankles. Two men were drizzling hot wax from burning candles onto her skin, but instead of the woman screaming in pain, she was moaning with desire.

After about ten minutes, her men led her to the next window. The woman on the table had small glass cups all over her body. Two were over her nipples, which were standing up as if the air had been pumped out of the cups. The next room had a sub and three Doms gathered onto a bed large enough to hold all of them. The sub was being triple penetrated. She had one man fucking her ass, another fucking her pussy and she was giving the third a blow job. With each scene, Justine became more aroused.

"Which scene did you like the best?" Derrick asked as her men led her back across the great room.

"I liked all of them, but I wasn't sure about the candle one."

"Wax play is very stimulating," Garth said. "The sub can't anticipate where the next drip will land since she is blindfolded. It's all about anticipation and sensation. The hot wax stimulates her nerve endings and can send her into subspace."

"Subspace is the optimum level of trust a Dom wants to achieve with his sub," Derrick added. "The endorphins running through her system, along with her arousal and the excitement, become so great that it's like the sub is floating on a cloud. She is only aware of her Dom or Doms and nothing else. It's one of the headiest experiences for all in play. The Dom's body is pumped up on adrenaline and control at achieving the highest peak their sub can undergo." Derrick helped her onto a bar stool.

"It usually takes a lot of trust from the sub and a very highly trained Dom for that to happen," Garth clarified. "I'd like for our first scene to be on the stage. Do you have any objections?"

"No, Master."

"Good. Do you want a drink of water before we begin?" Derrick asked.

"No thank you, Master."

Derrick and Garth each took a hand and led her toward the now-empty stage. She took a deep breath and then released it, trying to circumvent her nervousness. Once she was up on the stage, she kept her eyes on her men.

"Strip, sub," Derrick commanded.

Justine raised her arms and fumbled with the clasps of her corset. Her fingers were shaking so much it took her twice as long as it normally would to remove her top. Derrick took the top from her and dropped it on the floor off to the side. Next she removed her skirt until she was standing on the dais, totally naked except for the stilettos on her feet.

"Remove the shoes, baby," Garth directed.

Justine held onto Garth's arm as she stepped out of the shoes.

"Step up, Jusi." Derrick helped her up the small step until the front of her body was resting on the padded *X*. Garth lifted one of her arms while Derrick lifted the other and then wrapped them in wide, soft, padded cuffs. She gave a slight tug when they stepped back but couldn't move her arms at all.

"Spread your legs, baby," Garth commanded in a deep, husky voice that caused her insides to clench with desire.

Justine did as she was told and then her legs were also secured to the apparatus. The air moved behind her and she knew that her men had stepped back. She heard a zipper and knew that one of them was rummaging in the bag that Garth had brought with him from home. A shiver of nervous excitement traversed her spine and caused her to shudder.

"What is your safe word, sub?" Derrick asked in a deep, gravelly voice.

"Red, Master."

"And what is the word you will use if you want to take a break, baby?"

"Yellow, Master Garth."

"Very good, sub."

Smack.

Justine gasped at the heated tingle the hand caused on her ass.

Smack.

She whimpered when that one connected, because it was harder than the first one.

Smack, smack. Smack.

Her ass was on fire from their hands slapping her flesh, and although it hurt, it was also pleasurable. Each swat caused her now-naked pussy to vibrate and amped her libido up more.

"How are you doing, Jusi?" Master Derrick panted and she knew he was as turned on as she was.

"Good, Master Derrick."

Smack. Smack. Smack. Smack. Smack.

"Oh God."

"No talking, sub," Master Garth growled and swatted her ass again.

Smack. Smack.

Juices were leaking from her cunt in a continuous stream now, and she knew she wouldn't be able to take much more without climaxing,

Smack. Smack.

She could tell that her Masters were taking turns applying their hands to her ass because of the different ways their hands connected with her backside. Master Derrick brought his whole hand down on her flesh as did Master Garth, but Master Garth's wallops stung more. He seemed to kind of flick his wrist when he smacked her and it hurt more. Or that was what she imagined was happening, but she couldn't be sure since they were behind her.

With each whack of their hand, adrenaline spiked in her system. She began to feel as if she was floating, but all her attention was on the two Masters behind her. She felt the air moving every time they moved and anticipated each swat to her ass.

A hand gripped her hair and the slight stinging pain to her scalp turned her on even more. She looked up into Garth's hazel eyes with blurry vision.

"God, you're beautiful. You look so damn fucking sexy with your gorgeous body on display. I can't wait to make love with you, baby."

Master Garth slammed his mouth down on hers and she sobbed with hunger. She was so damn horny that one more slap to her ass would send her into ecstasy. The kiss they shared was long, hot, wet, and carnal. By the time Master Garth lifted his mouth, tears of emotion were tracking down her cheeks.

"I love you," she slurred. Her tongue felt so thick in her mouth. "I love you both so much."

"Yes." Garth released her hair and ran his hands all over her body.

"I'm going to make you come, baby. And then Derrick and I are going to get you down from there, take you into one of the rooms out back and fuck you until you're screaming."

"Please?" Justine was beyond pride and begged him.

"Please what, honey?" Derrick's hot breath caressed her ear as he whispered into it, causing her to shake with desire.

"Please make me come, Masters?"

"You are so damn perfect for us, Jusi. Do you know how much I love you?"

"No." She whispered her reply.

"You'll know before this night is through." Derrick kissed her neck and moved back.

Garth gripped her hair again. "I love you so fucking much, baby. I can't wait to sink my hard cock into that tight little cunt."

Garth placed a hard but chaste kiss on her mouth and moved out of sight. Justine rested her head on the edge of one of the padded arms and tried to regain her breath, but she was too turned on and the feat seemed impossible.

She wondered what was happening when they began to release her restraints but didn't ask as she didn't want to displease her Doms.

"Turn around, Justine," Garth commanded.

Justine turned until she was facing her men.

"Put your arms above your head, honey," Derrick directed and she did as ordered.

Her men restrained her once more, and this time she could see all the men and women watching the scene, but instead of turning her off, her body quivered with desire.

"You are so fucking perfect for us, baby. You love being on display like this, don't you?"

"Yes, Master Garth."

"Beautiful," Master Derrick whispered. "Your body is so goddamn perfect. I am going to spend the rest of my life learning what you like."

Justine was so full of love and contentment. She was home when she was with her men.

Garth leaned down and sucked a hard nipple into his mouth, causing her to cry out. He suckled strongly, almost to the point of pain, but it was really just intensely pleasurable. Derrick moved in on her other side and laved the tip of her other breast with his tongue. She tried to arch up into their touch, but when they had restrained her again they had added a strap across her hips, which prevented any movement. Never in her life had she felt such decadence and they hadn't even fucked her yet.

A large, warm hand separated her slick pussy lips and then fingers caressed through her wet folds. She mewled with delight and then sobbed when the fingers brushed over her engorged, sensitive, aching clit. Another hand ran up her thigh and then a finger was being pushed into her soaking cunt. She cried out as her men worked in tandem to bring her to climax.

"Yeah, honey," Derrick rasped, "that's it. Let us hear all those little noises of pleasure."

The finger in her pussy pumped in and out a few times and then withdrew. She was just about to protest, but the words died on her lips as two fingers pressed up inside her.

"We're going to make you come so hard, baby. Your juices are going to gush from your cunt. I don't want you to fight us. Trust us to bring you pleasure, Justine."

Justine had no idea what Garth was talking about but she trusted both of them. She closed her eyes and gave her body over to the two men she loved more than her own life. The fingers on her clit began to rub faster and faster and the ones pumping in and out of her vagina sped up, too.

Garth twisted his fingers without removing them from her pussy and slid them in and out but used the pads to caress her upper wall as if searching for something. He hit a spot inside her that made her buck and then he rubbed the tip of his fingers over that spot again and again while also giving a slight tugging motion.

Justine's womb ached with desire and the muscles in her vagina began to gather in, getting tauter and tauter. Liquid warmth traveled throughout her body, making her feel boneless, but at the same time her body was rife with tension. The fingers on her clit separated and then squeezed. She closed her eyes tightly and screamed as nirvana washed over her. Neither of her Masters stopped the movement of their fingers and just as she thought she was going to come down from her climax, they each did something that sent her flying again. Her body shook and quavered as the waning contractions of her pussy strengthened and fluid gushed out of her cunt in a great wave, wetting the hands giving her bliss, her thighs, and the floor below. A final wave wracked her body and then she slumped with satiation.

She felt another tremor when her Masters removed their fingers from her body and then worked quickly to release her from the restraints. Derrick wrapped her in a blanket and swept her up into his arms. She turned her head to see that Garth was already cleaning down the equipment and thanked someone when they brought him a mop and bucket filled with hot water and disinfectant. With a sigh she rested her head on his shoulder and snuggled up to Derrick. He carried her off to the other side of the dance floor and sat down with her in his lap.

"You were amazing, honey. Did you like your first taste of BDSM?"

"Yes," she sighed and pressed her nose into his neck. She loved the way her men smelled. Natural and musky with a hint of cologne. She couldn't get enough.

"Do you think you'd want to explore some more?"

Justine pushed up until she was looking into Derrick's brown eyes. "I want to do everything with the both of you."

"That's good, because we want to show it all to you."

Garth sat on the small sofa next to them and stroked a hand over her hair. "Are you ready, baby?"

She didn't need him to explain any more, since they had already told her they wanted to take her to a private room in the back of the club and make love with her.

"Yes. I can't wait."

Chapter Eleven

As Derrick carried Justine down the hallway, Garth opened the door that led into their room, which was set up much like a motel room, but with a large bed as the focal point at the center of the space. Derrick lowered her to her feet by the bed.

Justine's skin rose in goose bumps when he pulled the blanket from around her body and then he placed his hands on her shoulders and turned her toward the bed. She was just in time to see Garth pulling the covers and top sheet to the bottom of the bed.

Without speaking, she climbed into the middle of the mattress and lay down on her back. Her men kept their eyes on her as they began to remove their clothes. She would never get tired of seeing their thickly muscled arms or delineated chests and abs. When their hands moved to the waist bands of their jeans, she watched with bated breath as they undid their buttons and lowered their zippers. As if they had synchronized the action, both men pushed their jeans and form-fitting boxers from their hips and down their thighs.

She gasped at the first look of their hard cocks. Derrick's erection was thicker than average, but really long. It was long enough that the tip reached past his navel. The head was a dark red and she saw a drop of clear fluid glistening on the top. Her gaze moved to Garth's hard rod and she whimpered with trepidation and excitement. He wasn't as long as his brother, but he was thicker. His corona was a deep purple color and it moved slightly with every beat of his heart.

"Are you on any contraception, Justine?" Garth asked as he moved toward her and then climbed up next to her on her right side.

"No." She frowned, hoping that wasn't going to be a problem. "I've only had sex once and that was in the final year of high school."

Derrick made a rumbling sound deep in his chest and then picked up his pants from the floor. After rummaging in his pocket, he brought out what she presumed was a condom but then he unfurled it and she realized it was a whole strip of protection. He got on the bed on her left side and then looked at her.

"We've been tested since the last time we were with a woman and are both clean. Neither of us have ever had sex without using protection."

"That's good to know. Thank you. Why did you growl when I told you I've only been with one man, well boy, really?"

"I was surprised that such a beautiful, sexy woman hadn't had a relationship beyond school, but also pleased that you trust us enough to share your body with us."

"Enough talking," Garth growled and then turned her face toward him. "Your safe words still work in this room, baby. If we do anything to frighten you don't hesitate to use them. All right?"

"Okay."

Garth didn't waste another second. He leaned over and down and began kissing her, starting off slow and then deepening the connection of their mouths. His tongue pushed in between her lips and teeth, sliding along hers and then skimming the inside of her cheeks and up to tickle the roof of her mouth. She loved his taste and the way he kissed sent her inner flames shooting high. But when she felt Derrick move in closer and begin to caress his hands over her naked skin, she was close to shooting into the stratosphere.

When Garth released her mouth, she gulped in air, trying to calm her raging desire, but she should have known her two Doms wouldn't let her stay in control. Derrick licked across her nipple and then sucked it into her mouth. She cried out when he held it gently between his teeth and flicked the tip of his tongue across her nipple rapidly.

"Yes, baby," Garth panted, "let us hear all your pleasure."

Derrick released her nipple with soft, wet pop just as Garth began to nibble on her other breast. Derrick licked his way down over her ribs and stomach until he reached her mound. With a gentle nudge she spread her legs and then felt the mattress dip as he moved between her splayed thighs.

She felt his moist breath against her humid lips right before he slicked his tongue up through her wet folds. Without conscious thought, her hips arched up trying to get more of the exquisite sensations being bestowed on her. Garth growled against her breast and then sucked on her nipple firmly while placing a hand on her lower belly to hold her down. Derrick also put a hand on her hip and applied pressure to stop her from moving.

She moaned when Derrick's tongue lapped up her juices and then pressed against her clit, making her sensitive nub throb with need. Justine nearly screamed when he brought her aching pearl into his mouth and suckled firmly. When she thought she was just about to reach her peak, both men pulled back. Biting down on her lower lip was the only thing that stopped her from voicing her frustration.

The sound of a packet being ripped open made her realize that she had her eyes closed, and she lifted her weighted lids in time to see Derrick sheathing his cock with the condom.

"Are you ready for me, honey?"

"God, yes."

Derrick moved up close to her between her legs until the tip of his latex-covered cock touched her pussy. He pushed against her and although he wasn't as thick as Garth, her body still resisted.

"Relax, baby." Garth rubbed a soothing hand over her belly. "Let Derrick in."

Justine took a deep breath and released it slowly. That was enough to relax her tight muscles and the tip of his cock breached her vagina.

"Fuck! She's so fucking tight," Derrick said between clenched teeth. "Am I hurting you, Jusi?"

"No," she groaned. "Give me more, Derrick."

Derrick pushed in another inch and held still, giving her body time to adjust to the intrusion. He took his time pressing into her and then holding still again until he was buried all the way inside her.

"So goddamn good. You're unbelievably tight, hot, and wet." Derrick pulled out a couple of inches and then surged back in.

With each stroke, he increased the pace incrementally until his balls were slapping against her ass. Derrick's moan joined hers until they were both groaning almost continuously.

"I'm not gonna last, man. Help her over," he panted as he pushed his cock in until he bumped her cervix. Derrick slipped his arms beneath the crook of her knees and lifted her up until her hips left the bed. The different angle had the head of his cock rubbing over the sweet spot inside her.

Justine mewed when his cock once more bumped her womb, because that little bite of pain added to her joy. Garth reached down her body and began to lightly caress the tip of his finger on her clit. Molten lava traveled through her body while her muscles grew tauter and her toes began to curl under. Derrick pumped into her faster and faster and then Garth pinched her clitoris between two fingers and she went flying.

Her head tipped back and she opened her mouth on a breathless cry. The rapture swamping her was so strong she was left without any voice. Her muscles clenched and released and gripped and let go over and over. She was vaguely aware of the shout Derrick gave as he pressed into her one last time and then he froze. The muscles in his arms were under her hands and felt like warm steel. His body shook slightly and she knew he had found his release, too. Garth removed his hand from her pussy and shifted away when Derrick dropped down on top of her. His panting breaths were loud in her ear, but she had never heard a more rewarding sound.

Justine cherished the closeness with him and relished the weight of his body over hers. She loved him more in that moment than she had previously and knew her love would grow for each of her men the more time she spent with them. Derrick finally pushed up onto his arms, lifting his upper body from her.

"That was so special, Jusi. I've never felt anything like that before." Derrick kissed her on the lips and then gently withdrew from her body and collapsed on the bed beside her.

* * * *

"How are you feeling, baby? Are you sore?" Garth asked.

"No. I feel wonderful."

"Do you want more?"

"Hell yes."

Garth nearly slumped in relief. He'd been worried that she would be too tender to make love with him after having sex with Derrick. His cock was so hard he could probably break ice with it, and he'd been in danger of shooting off when Justine had reached climax. He reached for a condom and tore the pack open. After donning the prophylactic, he moved to cover her body with his. Using his arms to brace his weight, he leaned down and took her mouth with his. She tasted so good, he could have spent hours just kissing her. He released her mouth and kissed his way down her neck and bit into the tender spot where shoulder and neck met.

Justine cried out and arched up into him and he couldn't take it anymore. He had to have her and he had to have her now. He slipped his arms under her ass and squeezed her cheeks, aligned his cock to her pussy, and began to push into her. Garth was glad she was wet from her climax with Derrick, because he might have had trouble getting his cock inside her. He groaned when the crown breached her tight hole squeezing the life out of him.

Justine wrapped her arms around his neck and threaded her fingers into his hair. After massaging his scalp, her hand caressed over his shoulder and down his back. Garth rocked his hips, gaining depth with every forward thrust of his pelvis. He'd never felt anything as good as he was feeling right now. The women before Justine were nothing in comparison to being with the love of his life. He surged into her again and growled when he hit bottom. She was so fucking tight she was grasping him like a fist. No wonder Derrick had had trouble holding his climax back. He was having the same problem.

The base of his spine was starting to tingle and he knew if he kept pumping his hips, sliding his cock in and out of her, he would be lost. He had to make her come first. Shifting a little so he could reach further under her with his left arm, he touched the underside of his cock and gathered some of her cream and then he moved back up and tickled over her back entrance.

Justine went wild under him, bucking and sobbing as he continued fucking her. He applied more pressure until the tip of his finger passed her tight ring of muscle and began to surge in and out of her faster and faster. The tingling warmth at the bottom of his spine got stronger and he was about to go over. With the next thrust of his hips, he twisted a little so that his pubic bone hit her clit, and he pressed his finger further into her ass. Her internal muscles rippled around his cock and then she screamed as she reached climax.

Garth pumped into her twice more and then roared as his balls drew up and his sperm shot up his dick and spewed out the top of his cock. The only thing that would have topped the most powerful climax of his life would be if he had experienced it bareback.

He collapsed on top of her, but made sure not to crush her. Aftershocks still rocked her system, which caused his dick to pulse in answer. Garth vowed to himself that he would protect her with his last breath and that he would also spend the rest of his life loving her. It was on the tip of his tongue to ask her to marry them but it was way too soon for her. She'd only just got her head around being submissive to their Doms and had just really started the physical side of their relationship.

Maybe in a week or two she would be ready. God he hoped so.

* * * *

He'd followed them home from the office, but thanks to some research, he hadn't tried to breach the grounds. The place had state-of-the-art security and he wasn't about to alert anyone of his presence. The cops were already familiar with him and there was no way in hell he was going to give them an excuse to detain him for questioning.

That Bart asshole he'd worked over had said the girl had the drugs. Well, he didn't have to worry about that fucker anymore.

If he didn't find the drugs soon, then he was a dead man, but he would get the woman and keep her until he had the package.

He'd tie the bitch up and beat her until she gave him what he wanted and then he'd have a little fun before slitting her throat.

His patience paid off. He'd been sitting in his car for two and a half hours and was about to call it a night when headlights shone out through the wrought-iron gate as it began to open.

He waited until they'd followed the curve in the road before starting after them. Twenty minutes later the truck pulled into another driveway, which he drove past so as not to draw suspicion. He parked his car off the side of the road in a copse of trees and then hiked back on foot. There was a sign on the gate that read Club of Dominance. He rubbed his hands together and chuckled. It looked like the little bitch would like getting the tar beaten out of her. He could hardly wait to rough her up. It always got him excited to dominate a woman.

He headed back to his car and made a few phone calls while he drove back to their house. If there was a way to disable that security system without setting of any alarms then his good friend Travis would know.

Chapter Twelve

Justine snuggled up to Derrick while Garth drove the truck. It was the early hours of the morning and she was looking forward to getting into bed and falling asleep between her two men. They had each made love to her again and she was pleasantly sore from using muscles she hadn't used before, but she couldn't wait to do it all again. Tomorrow was Saturday and none of them had to go into work, so they could wake up by themselves without the annoying sound of an alarm.

Garth turned into the drive and pulled to a stop. "Fuck, it looks like we've had a power outage. The gate is wide open. This is the second time in three months that the power has gone out."

"Yeah, I don't like that anybody could drive in here whenever they feel like it. We're going to have to get a backup generator that will kick in if this happens again."

"Shit, I was going to do that, but I completely forgot about it. We've been so damn busy we've hardly had time to scratch ourselves."

"I hear you," Derrick replied. "I think it's time we got Matt and Luke out of the control room and gave them more responsibility. I want more time to spend with our woman."

"I understand that your business comes first, guys. I appreciate that you have to put in long hours to succeed."

"But that's it, Jusi, we've already succeeded and it's about time we scaled back our hours and shared the work load. We can hire more guards to watch the monitors. Luke and Matt know everything about the business, since they're partial owners and helped us set it up."

Garth smiled toward her and then put the stick in gear and drove toward the house.

"I don't like this, Garth." Derrick stared through the front windshield.

"Me either," he replied when he pulled the truck up close to the house. "Baby, I want you to stay in here until one of us comes out to get you, okay?"

"Okay."

Derrick and Garth got out of the truck, but before heading to the house, Garth opened the back door of the vehicle and unlocked a panel, which had been built into the floor. Behind the panel was a pair of handguns and a couple clips for each. Justine became nervous when Garth jammed a clip into one of the pistols and handed it to Derrick before loading one for himself. He closed the back door quietly and pointed to the lock, mouthing, "Lock the door."

She pushed the button down and felt a little better when the central locking secured all the doors. Derrick stalked toward the front door and Garth disappeared around the side of the house. The quiet made her breathing sound louder than normal and she could hear her own heartbeat in her ears. She was more on edge than she'd thought when she realized that she was panting.

A silhouette of a large man exited the front door and headed toward the truck. She sighed in relief that Derrick was coming for her. She unlocked the door and opened the passenger door.

"I'm glad you're back. I was beginning to—"

"Move over, now."

Justine opened her mouth to scream but nothing came out when she saw the gun pointed at her.

"Hurry up and move before I shoot you," he whispered in a raspy voice.

Justine was shaking so badly she felt uncoordinated and found it difficult to move. When she was in the driver's seat, she surreptitiously reached for the door handle.

"Don't." Cold metal was shoved hard into her temple. "Start the truck."

Justine automatically reached for the seat belt and put it on. Then with trembling fingers she turned the key in the ignition.

"Drive. Fast." He again pushed the tip of the gun painfully into her head.

Justine released the brake and put her foot on the accelerator. She was so scared that she applied too much pressure and the tires squealed on the concrete drive as she backed the truck up and turned it around and headed for the road. Just as she got to the end of the drive she glanced in the rearview mirror and saw Garth's and Derrick's shadows. She hoped they were calling the police. The gears ground as she shifted and the truck lurched forward but that was the least of her worries. She'd never seen the man sitting beside her before and had no idea why he was kidnapping her. Maybe if she got him talking he would stay calm and it would give her men more time to find her.

"Who are you?"

"Oh, so Bart didn't talk about his work colleagues? Why am I not surprised? Fucking asshole."

"What are you talking about?" Justine was still scared but some of the adrenaline that had swept through her was wearing off and she was able to change gears without the gearbox grinding.

"Bart was a drug dealer. He made a shitload of money while sponging off of you and your spineless brother."

"Don't you dare talk about Mark," Justine sobbed. "You didn't even know him."

"Who gives a shit?"

"What has all this got to do with you and why did you kidnap me?"

"Bart was supposed to deliver a package for me but it never got dropped off. He told me that you had it."

"What? That fucking asshole. I don't know anything. I didn't even like him. I only put up with him because he was a friend of my brother."

"Well, if you don't have the drugs and Bart definitely didn't, then where are they?"

"I have no idea." Fear caused another spike of adrenaline and her heart beat rapidly inside her chest. She tried to think where Bart might have left the drugs, but it was really hard to concentrate with a gun pointed at her. The only place that kept popping into her head was the house she shared with her brother and him. "He might have hidden them at the house."

"Then that's where we're going. Don't do anything to alert the cops or I'll put a bullet in your leg."

* * * *

Derrick heard the screech of tires out front and ran toward the door. He was just in time to see Garth's truck backing up and then fishtailing down the driveway with Justine at the wheel, but what nearly made his knees buckle was the shadowy frame of a large man in the passenger seat beside her, and if he had seen correctly, he was holding a gun to her head.

"Did you see who it was?" Garth snarled.

Derrick hadn't even heard his brother come up to him. He'd been concentrating on Justine.

"No."

"Was that a gun I saw against her head?"

"I think so."

"Fuck!" Garth roared and then fumbled in his pocket. Derrick pulled his cell phone out the same time his brother did. "I'm calling Gary Wade."

"I'll call 9-1-1." Derrick moved away from Garth so he could talk without being distracted. After calling in Justine's kidnapping he hurried back into the house so he could access the garage and headed to the manual override for the automatic garage door. It took him a couple of minutes but finally the door was high enough to get his truck out.

Garth jumped in through the passenger door after he backed up and then Derrick sent the truck careening down the drive.

"Gary's put out an APB on my truck. If the cops spot it, they'll call it in."

"Good."

"Gary was heading here and wanted us to wait for him."

"Fuck that," Derrick snarled. "I'm not sitting around doing nothing when the woman we love needs us."

"My thoughts exactly."

Derrick concentrated on the road as he pushed the truck to the limit. He wasn't slowing down for anything. He wanted Justine back in his arms and bed, safe and sound.

"Any idea where you're headed?"

"Yeah, Justine's house."

"You think that was Bart?"

"It's the only conclusion I can think of. He's going to take her somewhere familiar."

"Step on it, bro."

"If I go any faster, I'll roll the fucking truck."

"Sorry." Garth sighed. "I've never been so scared in my life."

"Me either."

* * * *

Justine drove past the house and then pulled in to the curb three houses down. She got out the driver's door and was about to run when the asshole grabbed onto her arm.

"Keep quite or I'll put a bullet in you. Your neighbors won't hear a thing because of the silencer."

She looked at the gun and saw what he said was true. He must have put that on while she was driving. She was too scared to be very observant. A hard tug on her arm nearly made her fall, but she was able to save herself. His grip was bruising but she wasn't about to give him the satisfaction of crying out. He propelled her up the side of the house and around to the back door. Justine didn't have her purse so she had no key to get inside. She hoped that her neighbors would hear if the asshole had to kick the door in but she found out moments later that he didn't need to.

He shoved her against the side of the house and kept the gun pressed against her belly and then reached into his pocket and withdrew a credit card from his wallet. "This should do it." Looking her in the eye, he smiled at her and Justine felt her skin crawl. She was in deep shit.

What if Bart hadn't hidden the drugs inside? Would he kill her then? Adrenaline surged again, causing her limbs to shake and feel weak.

He slid the credit card between the crack of the door and wooden door jamb and the door began to swing open. He chuckled and grabbed her arm again.

"Piece of cake. Get inside." He gave her a shove and let go of her arm.

Justine had to get away. If she could make it to the kitchen, she would be able to get a knife and hopefully defend herself or do a lot of damage to him. *Yeah right, Justine. Can you dodge bullets, too?*

"Which was Bart's room?"

Justine pointed toward the hallway off the kitchen and he shoved her again. "Lead the way, bitch."

On shaking legs she led the way and prayed he wouldn't shoot her in the back. Once inside Bart's room, she stepped to the side so he could enter.

He pointed to the chair in the corner. "Sit down there and don't fucking move."

She sat, grateful to be off her wobbly limbs, and prayed that her men would find her. Surely this would be the first place they looked for her. They ran their own security business and were smart men. Garth and Derrick would have called the police to alert them of her kidnapping. Yes, they wouldn't give up until they found her.

The asshole began searching the room and when he couldn't find what he was looking for he began destroying things. He smashed drawers, pulled the bedding and mattress from the bed and swept the lamp from the bedside table to send it crashing to the floor. When each search was futile, he became more angry and aggressive.

She glanced toward the bedroom door and weighed up her chances of escaping without getting a bullet in her back. She wasn't Superman and had no superpowers and she was too scared to take the chance. No one was faster than a speeding bullet.

* * * *

Thirty minutes later, Derrick turned onto Justine's street and pulled over five houses down from hers.

"Thank God you remembered what her address was from her job application."

"Yeah," Derrick replied and then checked the clip in his gun. "Let's go."

"Wait." Garth placed a hand on his arm to stop him opening the door. "Let me send Gary a text first. Then he knows where we are if anything goes down."

Derrick gave him a nod and then waited impatiently for Garth to send the message. He checked his phone and made sure it was on silent and then led the way down the sidewalk with Garth on his heels.

The curtains were drawn, but Derrick noticed the glow of a light coming from a side window. There was definitely someone here. He hoped it was Justine and that she was unharmed.

He didn't bother going to the front door, because he knew it would be locked and he didn't want to alert whoever was inside to their presence. They crept down the side of the house and he ducked under the window where the light was coming from. Once he was on the other side, he straightened against the wall of the house and peeked in through the slit in the curtain.

A strange man was searching the bedroom, but he couldn't see Justine. He took off around the back with Garth on his heels. He reached out for the back door handle and turned it.

They were in luck. The door was unlocked.

* * * *

Garth followed Derrick into the kitchen off the back door and scanned the room. He didn't hear anything and only hoped that Justine was okay. A crash from the other side of the house made him flinch, but then he hurried toward where the sound had come from with Derrick following behind.

He flicked the safety off his gun and slowed his steps. The last thing he wanted to do was alert the perp of their presence by becoming sloppy. His heart was nearly pounding out of his chest with fear for his woman and adrenaline for the upcoming confrontation. When he came to the room the light was emanating from, he hugged the wall and then with care moved his head forward slightly so he could see what was going on in the room.

The fucker wasn't Bart, but that didn't matter. All that mattered was getting Justine out of danger. A loud bang and then small thuds emitted from the room as the prick threw a drawer to the floor. Garth ducked back when the guy spun around and prayed he hadn't been spotted.

"Where the fuck is it, bitch?"

"I d–don't kn–know." Justine's voice quavered with fear.

Garth heard the guy walking across the floor and knew his time had run out. He slid inside the doorway just as the asshole reached Justine. The gun in his hand was lifting and Garth knew if he didn't shoot now, then it would be too late. Without any hesitation Garth aimed and fired. His aim was true. He put a bullet right between the fucker's eyes and a stunned expression crossed the bastard's face as he died where he stood and then fell to the ground.

He rushed over to Justine, stepping over the fucker's body, and scooped her from the chair. Her eyes were glazed over and she was shaking, but she was alive and unharmed. He carried her out of the bedroom and down the hall to the living area but then changed direction toward the kitchen when he saw the blood stain on the floor where her brother must have died.

Garth sat down in a chair and hugged her tight. Derrick squatted down beside them and rubbed up and down her back, offering comfort. Justine buried her face against his chest and cried. Great heart-wrenching sobs shook her body.

When she finally began to settle, she pushed against his chest and sat up.

"Thank you. You both saved my life," she sobbed.

"Come here, honey, I need a hug."

Garth passed her over to Derrick, who stood up and hugged her tight. "I was so damn scared, Jusi. I love you, honey."

"I love you, too."

Garth moved in close until his chest was up against her body and he kissed her temple. "Love you, babe." His voice was more raspy than usual and he had a tight lump in his chest. He hoped to never have to go through something like that again. He felt like ten years had been taken off his life.

"I love you, too."

They all jumped when another male voice interrupted their celebration.

"I should lock you two up for not waiting for me." Detective Gary Wade walked in through the back door. "But I'm glad you didn't and were able to save your woman."

Garth shifted until he was standing beside Derrick and Justine. "Baby, this is our friend, Detective Gary Wade. Gary, the love of our lives and sub, Justine Downey."

"Ma'am. Why don't we all take a seat and you can tell me what happened?"

Derrick sat with Justine in his lap this time. By the time she had finished her statement, forensics and the coroner had arrived and Justine was exhausted. She was yawning every other minute and could barely keep her eyes open.

"Okay, we're done. Take your woman home."

Garth hadn't heard sweeter words and was happy he would be able to spend the rest of his life loving his woman.

Chapter Thirteen

Justine had wondered what had happened to Bart until Gary Wade visited one night a week after her abduction and told her his body had been found in a Dumpster in an alley in town. Although she wouldn't have wished him dead, she wasn't sorry for what had happened to him. She figured he got his just desserts for killing her brother. The asshole who had kidnapped her, Allen Lombardo, was well known to the DEA for his involvement in the drug world, but they hadn't been able to arrest him since they had no evidence. They wouldn't have to worry about him again.

The day after her abduction she had buried her brother and her men had stood at her side giving her all the support and love she needed to get through such a difficult, emotional day. Garth and Derrick had been her rocks and she couldn't imagine not having them in her life now that she had finally found them.

It had been two weeks since the incident and Justine had spent every night loving and sleeping between her Doms. Her men had talked to Matt and Luke, and the Plant brothers were once more taking on more of the workload in their security business, for which she was thankful, because she got to spend more quality time with her Doms.

They had taken her to the club twice over the past two weeks and each time she went she was eager for more. It was Friday night and she was hoping they would be taking her to Club of Dominance again. She was so excited by that thought her pussy clenched and cream leaked out onto her inner thighs. Justine had just finished showering and was in the process of picking out some clothes to wear.

"Don't bother getting dressed, baby." Garth's voice was unexpected and she startled. She hadn't heard him come in. Turning to look at him, she hoped he didn't see the disappointment in her eyes. "Just put your robe on."

"Okay." She sighed with disenchantment and reached for her robe. After pulling it on she walked over to him and placed her hand in the one he held out to her and then followed him out to the living room.

Derrick was sitting on the sofa and looked up as she entered. His eyes brightened and she could see the love he felt for her.

"Take a seat, baby." Garth pointed toward the sofa, so she did what he ordered.

Derrick pushed off from the couch and began to pace in front of her. He looked nervous and she wondered what was going on. She shifted her gaze to Garth and saw he was just as tense, but he was looking at her with so much emotion in his eyes that tears pricked the back of hers.

Garth nodded to Derrick and Derrick nodded back. She began to get a little worried but wasn't concerned for their relationship. Justine trusted these two men more than she had ever trusted anyone in her life.

"What…"

Garth and Derrick held a hand out, palm up, halting her speech. "No talking until we've finished, Justine," Garth commanded in his firm Dom voice. She was about to answer back, since they weren't in the bedroom or doing a scene, but the pleading look in Garth's eyes made her pause. She nodded in acquiescence.

Her men knelt down in front of her and each took a hand in theirs.

"Justine, I was only half alive until you came into my life. You have given me joy, love, and a future. I love you, babe." Garth turned to Derrick.

"Jusi, you are my heart and home and I couldn't breathe without you. You're the love of my life, honey."

"We love you so much," the men said together. "Will you marry us?"

Justine's heart overflowed with love and tears streaked down her face. Her heart was so full that when she opened her mouth to reply, the words wouldn't come. The hands on her tightened and she saw the uncertainty in their eyes. That they doubted her answer only made her love them more.

She closed her mouth and cleared her throat. "I was only existing before you both came into my life. I didn't realize how much I was missing. You've both shown me how to open my heart and my mind. I would be lost without you by my side.

"I would be honored to marry you."

"Thank God," Garth muttered and pulled her from the couch down onto his lap. Derrick reached into his shirt pocket and pulled a small box from it and then opened it. Inside was a beautiful two-carat diamond ring with two smaller diamonds embedded in the band.

"Oh my. It's gorgeous."

"Not as gorgeous as you, honey." Derrick pulled the ring from the box and slid it onto her left ring finger.

"I love you guys. Please don't ever change."

"We won't, baby." Garth kissed her on the top of her head and Derrick leaned forward to kiss her on the cheek. They helped her stand and stood as well. Then they folded their arms over their chests and gave her their Dom stare. "Strip."

Justine didn't hesitate. She reached for the belt tied around her waist and released it and then slid the robe from her shoulders and tossed it behind her to land on the sofa.

"Get into position, sub," Derrick commanded in his deep, gravelly Dom voice.

A shiver traversed her spine, her breasts swelled, and her nipples hardened. Moisture formed between her legs, and as she slowly got in the "slave position" they had shown her, her slick folds slipped together.

"Good girl," Garth praised. He unfolded his arms and stripped his T-shirt over his head, then his hands went to the buckle on his belt and he yanked it open. Derrick had also started undressing and she flicked her gaze from one hot, sexy man to the other as they removed their clothes.

As if they had choreographed the move, her men stepped forward while they fisted their cocks and they began to pump their hands up and down their erections. Pre-cum glistened on both tips and she licked her lips in anticipation.

Garth reached out with his free hand and gripped the hair at the back of her neck. "That's right baby, get those lips nice and moist so my cock can slide in and out of your sexy mouth."

When he pushed his hips forward, she opened her mouth and swirled her tongue around the mushroom-shaped head, eliciting a groan from him. "Suck me, Justine."

She separated her lips and took the head into her mouth and sucked firmly on the tip of his cock.

"Fuck, baby, your mouth is amazing," he panted.

Justine took him in as far as she could and as she withdrew, she hollowed her cheeks out and lightly scraped her teeth along his shaft and then released him with a slurp. She dove for Derrick's cock and bobbed her head up and down a few times, causing him to moan with pleasure.

"I can't take it," Derrick rasped. "I'm too triggered. I want inside her now."

Garth tugged her hair, pulling her mouth away from Derrick's cock, making her whine with frustration. She had wanted to get them off with just the use of her mouth.

"You can do that another time, baby, but right now we need to be buried deep inside your body." Garth let go of her hair, grasped her upper arms, and pulled her to her feet. He didn't give her time to get steady, but swept her up into his arms and headed for their bedroom.

She let out a shriek when she went flying through the air but laughed when she landed on the soft mattress. Her two Doms literally jumped onto the bed with her and then they were all over her. Garth dove between her legs and ravaged her pussy, licking, sucking, nipping, and slurping until she was on the edge of climax.

Derrick sucked on one nipple while pinching the other between his finger and thumb. He lifted his mouth while running a hand up and down her body from chest to belly. He splayed his hand wide over her stomach and stared deeply into her eyes.

"I can't wait to see you rounded with our child. There is nothing sexier than a pregnant woman."

Tears leaked from her eyes as she stared into Derrick's emotive brown ones and she swallowed around the lump of emotion in her throat. "I would love to have your babies." She looked down her body to gaze at Garth. He'd stopped eating out her pussy when Derrick had made his statement. A sheen of moisture formed in his eyes and she knew he was as overcome with emotion as she. They both were. She caught Derrick blinking as he tried to hold back his feelings.

"Do you mean that?" Garth asked.

"Yes."

"Hot damn." Derrick's words lightened the mood. "Then let's make a baby."

Between her two Dom's she was rolled onto her side so that she was facing Derrick. She knew what they were about to do and shivered with excitement. Her men had spent the last two weeks preparing her for this moment, and she couldn't wait to have them both inside her.

A pop sounded behind her and she knew Garth had just opened the bottle of lube. Derrick was on his side in front of her and he leaned over and took her mouth. He ate at her lips and thrust his tongue into her mouth. She moaned with desire as he swept his tongue around every inch of her interior. When cold, wet fingers slid in between the crack of her ass, she pushed her hips back, begging for more.

A firm slap landed on her butt cheek and then Garth's firm voice sent another shudder wracking through her. "Don't move, sub."

Justine mewled deep in her throat when Garth's finger began to breach her anus. Her flesh goose bumped and another shiver traveled up her spine. Derrick caressed down her body and then he slid his fingers through her moisture-covered pussy lips. He rimmed her pussy hole, gathering her cream and then lightly rubbed over her throbbing clit. She sucked on his tongue trying to portray her desperation to have her men loving her.

Garth pressed his finger into her rectum as far as it would go and she pulled away from Derrick's mouth to gasp out her frustration when he removed it. But then he was back with two fingers and the slight bite of burning pain enhanced her pleasure. Garth had three fingers in her ass, spreading them to stretch her out. He pulled them out, and as one arm slid under her head his other gripped her upper hip.

"Are you ready, baby?"

"Yes. Please hurry."

"What do you want, honey?" Derrick whispered through panting breaths while applying pressure to her clit.

"I want you to fuck me. Please?"

"Yes, baby. Stay nice and relaxed for me."

Garth lifted his hand from her hip and used it to lift the cheek of her ass. The crown of his cock pushed against her rosette and she concentrated on her breathing, trying to stay relaxed. The burning as he entered her back entrance was much more intense than anything she'd felt and she reached out to clutch Derrick's arm.

"Easy, honey. Stay nice and calm. We are going to give you so much pleasure." Derrick scooted down the bed until his head was level with her chest and he sucked a nipple into his mouth, which helped to distract her from the pressure on her asshole.

The tip of Garth's dick popped through her tight opening and he held still, giving her time to adjust to the intrusion. When her inner muscles relaxed, he began to rock his hips, gaining a little depth each time. She sighed with relief when she finally felt his hips cradling her ass from behind.

"You feel so fucking good, baby. You're squeezing me tighter than a fist," he panted. "Hurry the hell up, Derrick. I'm not gonna last long."

Derrick released her nipple and moved back up the bed. He lifted her thigh up over his hip, aligned his cock with her cunt and began to press forward. With Garth's penis in her ass, she felt every ridge and vein caressing her internal walls as Derrick slowly but surely forged his way inside her. When his corona bumped into her womb she groaned with joy.

Justine was packed full of cock and loved how her two men made her feel, but she needed more. She wasn't given the chance to voice her desire because just then Garth withdrew a couple of inches and then pushed back in. As he shoved forward, Derrick withdrew to the tip of his hard rod and then he pressed forward. With each movement of their hips they increased the speed incrementally until their flesh was slapping against her.

Nerve endings she'd never been aware of came to life, and her pleasure was enhanced two fold. Liquid warmth traveled through her blood stream, causing cream to leak from her pussy and tension to permeate her muscles. Her womb ached, but in a good way, and her cunt rippled around Derrick's cock. The friction of Garth's cock stroking in and out of her ass caused the tightness inside to coil stronger and stronger. The pressure was so great she couldn't speak and barely drew enough breath.

And then Garth nipped her shoulder. That small bite of pain was enough to send her hurtling up into the stratosphere as rapture consumed her. She shook and shuddered, her cunt contracting strongly and wildly as her men pounded in and out of her holes.

Justine screamed as bliss swamped her entire body and flashes of light formed before her eyes.

Garth yelled while gripping her hip firmly and pushed forward one more time before he froze. His cock pulsed inside her ass as he spilled his seed. Derrick pumped his hips twice more and butted against her cervix and he shouted. His dick twitched inside her as his cum spumed out, filling her pussy.

Justine slumped between her men, still impaled on their cocks, and tried to get her breathing under control. Her men were in the same condition, which made her smile.

"You're so special, Jusi. Love you, honey."

"You're our everything, baby." Garth kissed her shoulder and then gently withdrew from her ass, making them both groan.

"How about a soak in the spa bath, Jusi?"

"I don't think I can move."

"You don't have to." Garth got off the bed and lifted her away from Derrick. She giggled when he groaned.

"The best thing I ever did was apply for the job to be your assistant."

"Damn straight," Garth replied gruffly.

"Bet you didn't think you'd end up with two Doms." Derrick smirked at her as he entered the bathroom after her and Garth. "Just like we never imagined having a sub of our own to love."

"No, I had no clue what I was getting myself into." She stroked Garth's cheek and then reached out and did the same to Derrick. "But there is no other place I would rather be."

THE END

WWW.BECCAVAN-EROTICROMANCE.COM

ABOUT THE AUTHOR

My name is Becca Van. I live in Australia with my wonderful hubby of many years, as well as my two children.

I read my first romance, which I found in the school library, at the age of thirteen and haven't stopped reading them since. It is so wonderful to know that love is still alive and strong when there seems to be so much conflict in the world.

I dreamed of writing my own book one day but, unfortunately, didn't follow my dream for many years. But once I started I knew writing was what I wanted to continue doing.

I love to escape from the world and curl up with a good romance, to see how the characters unfold and conflict is dealt with. I have read many books and love all facets of the romance genre, from historical to erotic romance. I am a sucker for a happy ending.

For all titles by Becca Van, please visit
www.bookstrand.com/becca-van

Siren Publishing, Inc.
www.SirenPublishing.com

Lightning Source UK Ltd.
Milton Keynes UK
UKOW03f2108161213

223136UK00014B/822/P